DUCK!

The ball came right at batter Robbie Belmont's head!

Robbie hit the dirt. The pitch whooshed through the space where his head had just been. Robbie picked himself up, brushing the dirt off his uniform. The beanball had left him burning with anger.

Robbie used his anger. He took his stance again, steady as ever, only now his body was poised to cut loose.

The next pitch was a low outside curve. Robbie wouldn't have cared if it were a foot over his head. He was pumped. Every ounce of power he had went into his swing. Every worry and fear, all his frustration and anger exploded into that furious but fully controlled swing.

GARY CARTER'S
IR⊕N MASK

TRIPLE PLAY

by Robert Montgomery

Troll Associates

Library of Congress Cataloging-in-Publication Data

Montgomery, Robert, (date)
   Triple play / by Robert Montgomery; illustrated by Ralph Reese.
     p.   cm.—(Gary Carter's iron mask; 3)
   Summary: Eighteen-year-old Robbie Belmont's final year as catcher
for Riverton High's baseball team holds many distractions, as he
finds himself torn between two girls and must decide whether to
attend college or go directly into the major leagues.
   ISBN 0-8167-1990-X (lib. bdg.)   ISBN 0-8167-1991-8 (pbk.)
   [1. Baseball—Fiction.]   I. Reese, Ralph, ill.   II. Title.
III. Series: Montgomery, Robert, 1946-   Gary Carter's iron mask;
3.
PZ7.M76845Tr   1991
[Fic]—dc20   89-20179

10 9 8 7 6 5 4 3 2 1

INTRODUCTION

by Gary Carter

What is the rarest achievement in baseball? That's a question that can start a lot of arguments. In the major leagues, there are records that may never be broken. Among them are Nolan Ryan's more than 5,000 career strikeouts as a pitcher, Henry Aaron's 755 career home runs, and Ty Cobb's lifetime batting average of .367.

But those records were achieved over lengthy periods. There are other baseball feats that occur in the span of a single game. Consider the perfect game, a pitcher's ultimate dream, achieved just fourteen times in the history of the major leagues.

Rarer still, however, is the unassisted triple play. Only nine have ever been achieved in the majors, and one of those was in the *nineteenth* century. An unassisted triple play is an event most baseball lovers will never get to see in the major leagues. *That's* how rare it is!

There's no way really to practice for a triple

play. You just have to be ready for it when the chance comes along. But how do you get ready for something that happens less than once every ten years?

When it happens, there's virtually no time to stand back and think of what you're going to do next. That's because your thinking should have been done ahead of time, *before* the ball was even hit. It's called "mental preparation" or "staying focused." You just can't daydream out there, nor can you take it easy—ever.

Some people say an unassisted triple play is a matter of luck. That may be so—up to a point. Remember, there have been other occasions in baseball where a player had the chance for one— and missed it. It doesn't take much for a near-miss, either. Taking a split second too long to decide what to do next with the ball can make all the difference. Yes, luck's involved, but so are hard work and sound baseball instincts. You seldom get the one without the other two.

Of course, those aren't instincts that anyone is born with. They're acquired through years of watching and playing the game, years of studying it. They come from understanding the rules and goals of baseball and from concentrating on the action during the game.

Concentrating while out on the ball field is one of the biggest problems Robbie Belmont faces in this book. He has a lot on his mind, a lot that can and does distract him. There is the serious distraction of his dad's strange illness. And there remains a tough decision to make on what to do after high school, rapidly coming to a close for him.

Like most good baseball coaches, Gus Franklin does everything he can to help Robbie stay focused and alert. But in the end, it's up to Robbie. Only he can do it.

Come to think of it, the same is true for anyone.

Chapter One

Robbie Belmont stepped up to the plate. It was the first time he had gone to bat for his high-school team in two years. His last time up, he had hit a grand slam. With one swat, Robbie had taken his team from three runs down to a stunning 5–4 victory in the state championship. The memory of that was still sweet. But it seemed so long ago, almost as if it had happened in another century. Robbie had missed all of last season because of an injury.

That was then, this is now, thought Robbie, trying to concentrate at the plate. It felt good to be playing again. He was batting fourth, the cleanup spot, for the Riverton High School Tigers. It was his senior year, and this was the first inning of Riverton's opening game of the season.

The other team was the Hanover Falcons. Robbie had never batted against their pitcher before. His name was Danny Stewart. He looked strong and confident.

Stewart went into a half wind-up. He looked over at the runner on third, Ty Williams. Ty was the Tigers' star shortstop and leadoff hitter. He was a brash junior who never stopped hustling. He had hit the first pitch thrown to him for a single to center. Then he stole second base on the second pitch, and third base on the third pitch! But the next two batters, Riverton right fielder Abbie Jacobs and left fielder Dennis Wu, had struck out. It was up to Robbie to bring Ty home.

Stewart pitched with a violent sidearm motion. He fell to the right of the mound as he threw. At first, the ball seemed to be heading outside. But then it bent in and up through the heart of the strike zone.

Robbie swung and nicked the ball to the backstop. The pitch's rising hop had surprised Robbie. "Foul! Strike one!" called the umpire.

Robbie's baseball skills had gotten rusty since his injury. He had hurt himself during a pickup basketball game. Someone had hacked Robbie's thumb while trying to steal the ball from him. Robbie called time and walked around shaking his right hand for a while.

But he continued to play. Later in the game, he swung his arm around, trying to get a rebound. The same sore thumb smashed against the pole that held the backboard.

The x-rays showed three breaks at the base of

the thumb. For two months Robbie wore a cast. It wrapped around his thumb and went up to his elbow.

During that time, the Riverton Tigers won their division. Ty Williams was sensational. He fielded whatever his glove touched, and scored at least one run a game. And Bill "Wire" Wirick pitched impressively. The tall hurler was much stronger and fifteen pounds heavier than the year before.

Wire's pitching almost won the league championship for the Tigers. He pitched a no-hitter against the Fulton Bucks, but they still managed to score an unearned run. The quiet Tiger bats couldn't get even one run. They lost, 1–0, ending their season. There would be no league, county, regional, or state championships for Riverton. It was the Tigers' shortest baseball season since Robbie began high school.

Robbie took one last practice swing as Danny Stewart went into his wind-up. There was nothing wrong with Robbie's thumb now. His swing felt great. Stewart's sidearm pitch shot high and inside. Robbie's head flinched back. Then the ball curved, taking Robbie by surprise. He still could swing, but he was too off balance to hit cleanly. Robbie let it pass. "Stee-rike two!" said the umpire.

This guy is good, thought Robbie. He stepped out of the batter's box. Even though he had two strikes against him, Robbie wasn't worried about striking out. He loved to hit. He'd been hitting better than ever during preseason practice.

6

The Tigers were not the home team, but there was a solid section of Riverton fans. They were cheering loudly for Robbie to hit for extra bases. It was the long ball that the Tigers had lacked last season. Robbie stepped into the box determined to show everyone that power was back in the Tiger line-up.

He expected Stewart to waste the next pitch, to tempt him to swing at a bad ball. Sure enough, it was *very* tempting. Stewart's pitch sped toward the low inside corner, Robbie's favorite hitting zone. But the ball's big hop made it bend too far inside. Robbie checked his swing. "Ball," said the umpire.

"Come on, Robbie! Just meet the ball!"

There was no mistaking that voice. It was Melinda Clark, calling out from her seat next to the Riverton dugout. Melinda and Robbie had known each other as long as either could remember. They had grown up together on the same street.

Melinda was a math and computer wiz. She had gotten interested in baseball a few years ago. That's when she started dating the team's equipment manager, Josh Kenny. She began keeping team statistics. Then she fed them into a computer program she invented. Coach Gus Franklin came to depend on the things her stat sheets pointed out. She also did scouting reports and sometimes videotaped practices and games.

Last year, at Robbie's urging, the team voted her an official member of the team. So now she wore a Tiger uniform, with the number "1" on the back. She could sit on the bench, but liked the view better in the stands.

When she called out for Robbie to "meet the ball," she reminded him of something. A long ball wasn't necessary. A hit to score Ty from third was the main thing.

Robbie had needed the reminder. He'd been thinking of impressing the crowd instead of playing winning ball. He just had to connect cleanly, not kill the ball.

With two strikes, Robbie inched closer to guard the plate. Stewart's next sidearm pitch was a curve that snaked into the dirt for ball two. The Falcon catcher, Dale Davis, stopped it by throwing his whole body on top of it. It bounced off his stomach. Ty dashed two steps toward home. The catcher quickly picked up the ball. Ty scooted back to third.

"Good stop," Robbie said to the Falcon catcher. Dale Davis grunted his thanks. He knew Robbie was a catcher, too. They both appreciated what it took to block a wild pitch.

Robbie was a very different young man now than when he was a freshman. So much had happened since then! When Robbie looked back on how he played baseball as a fourteen-year-old, it seemed so simple. All he had to do was walk up to the plate, watch the ball come in, and *hit* it. Now, at seventeen, it seemed he had more things on his mind when he walked up to the plate. It wasn't as easy to focus on the game as it used to be.

Right now, thoughts of his parents ran through Robbie's head. Neither Simon nor Ellen Belmont were at the game today to watch Robbie play. Robbie's mother had taken his father to an eye doctor.

Last month, St. Simon Belmont had a long bout with the flu. He recovered, but a few days later he started having trouble seeing clearly. At times, his vision got so blurry that Robbie had to drive the car for him. Their regular family doctor didn't know the cause. That's why Simon was taken to a special eye doctor today.

Robbie missed his parents' sitting in the stands. His father was usually quiet, but his mother often cheered loud and long. Ellen Belmont knew how much the game of baseball meant to her son. A champion swimmer in college, she understood the feeling that flooded through an athlete during competition.

Robbie was thinking about all this, but especially about his father, as the Hanover pitcher wound up. The pitch whooshed by Robbie, who stood motionless with the bat on his shoulders.

There was a moment of silence from the umpire. Robbie and the Hanover catcher turned around to hear what he'd call.

"Ball three," said the umpire, as if it weren't important.

Robbie had been holding his breath and now let it out. His heart was pounding. He had almost been called out on strikes his first time up in two years!

When Danny Stewart heard the call, he glared at the umpire for a few seconds. Then he asked the catcher to throw the ball back. Stewart made no protest. He was smart enough not to make an enemy of the man who was calling his pitches.

"C'mon, Robbie! Pound this guy!" yelled Ty, taking a walking lead off third base. As Ty slowly kept walking farther from the bag, he called out to Stewart, "I'm going in, pitcher! Just watch me!" Ty kept walking slowly, daring Stewart to pick him off. But the Hanover pitcher stood there patiently. He didn't throw to third or home. Finally, Ty had to stop walking. One more inch and Stewart could pick him off.

Robbie stepped out of the box. Ty quickly jogged back to the bag.

After taking another deep breath, Robbie stepped back into the batter's box. He dug in, planting his back foot firmly and putting his front foot closer to the plate than his back foot. Robbie aimed his front shoulder at the pitcher. He lifted his back elbow. His bat pointed straight up in the air.

Ty took a regular lead off third base this time. He stood far enough to make Stewart pay attention to him, but close enough to beat a pick-off throw.

Stewart gave Ty a hard look. Then he began falling toward the third-base line, making his usual sidearm delivery. Robbie's eyes never left the ball as it hopped in. Suddenly, the old childhood knowledge of how to hit came back. *There's the ball! Hit it!*

His swing whipped around smoothly. The ball hit the fat of the bat. The Hanover center fielder backpedaled, then turned and ran after the ball. It bounced once before hitting the fence. Ty scored easily, and Robbie tore around first and headed for second. The Tiger fans were on their feet, screaming. Their favorite power hitter was *back*!

Robbie made it to second base standing up. Hanover's relay man was just now taking the throw from the center fielder. Robbie stood on second and tipped his hat to the cheering fans. He saw Melinda Clark aiming her video camera at him. There was a wide smile on her face. Robbie smiled, too. He felt like a fish that had been returned to the sea. It was great to be back.

Chapter Two

Batting fifth for Riverton was catcher-turned-first baseman Eddie Mosely. Last year, when Robbie was out with a broken thumb, Eddie had filled in as the Tigers' starting catcher. He had played well, hitting a solid .292 and catching confidently. At the end of last season, Eddie was named second-team all-league catcher.

Robbie and Eddie never really got along together. There were times during Robbie's freshman year when the two came close to fistfighting. This past preseason, the pair got into some heated competition for the starting catcher's job. Robbie's greater hitting power and stronger throwing arm eventually won out. But it had not been easy for him.

Eddie wasted no time in knocking Robbie home from second base. As fast as Stewart's first pitch came in, it went out a lot faster. Eddie slugged a hard single up the middle, making the score 2–0. But Eddie was left stranded on first base when

Stewart got Riverton third baseman Sam Thorne to pop up for the third out.

His second time up, with no one on and two out, Robbie swung for the fences. But he hit under the ball and only sent a high fly to the left fielder. His third time up, in the fifth inning, he hit a sacrifice fly to deep center. Todd Murphy, the quiet Tiger second baseman, easily tagged up and scored from third.

For five innings, Bill Wirick's pitching had been awesome. The sight of Wire staring in from the mound for the signal was enough to scare all but the best batters. And even the best batters had trouble with Wire's burning speed and different pitching motions. Wire's days as a string-bean pitcher were long gone. He now knew how to put the solidly packed weight of his tall frame into every pitch.

But in the bottom of the sixth inning, the fire began to leave his fast ball. His old control problem came back. Two walks and a wild pitch put Hanover runners on second and third. Then, Falcon catcher Dale Davis hit a Wire fast ball for a two-run single. That cut the Tigers' lead to 3–2.

In the seventh inning, Wire walked the first batter. The Tiger third baseman, Sam Thorne, trotted to the mound. Sam played hard but was an easygoing guy. He said a few words of encouragement to Wire and walked back to his position. Sam was good at settling pitchers down.

Robbie got into his catcher's crouch. He put down one finger to signal for a fast ball. The

Falcon batter stood far away from the plate. This made the outside corner seem like a good place to aim for. But Robbie had learned something about batters who stand far from the plate. They *liked* outside pitches. It was *inside* pitches they didn't like. That's why they stood so far from the plate! Robbie held his target on the inside corner.

Right before Wire released the ball, the batter stepped toward the plate to cover the outside corner. Wire threw the fast ball in tight, right where Robbie wanted. The batter hit it on the handle of the bat.

The ball dribbled toward the mound. Wire charged in and barehanded it. Robbie had taken a step in front of the plate to see the action better. He thought Wire might have a good chance to throw the lead runner out at second, but wasn't sure. "First, Wire!" he called, choosing the safe out at first.

But Wire ignored Robbie's call. He whirled and threw to Ty Williams covering second. The runner was out by a foot. Ty threw to first, hoping for the double play. But the runner beat the throw.

Robbie called time and stormed to the mound. "I called for you to throw to first, Wire!" he snapped at his pitcher. "You were lucky this time, but maybe next time you won't be! I'm supposed to call those plays! You have to trust me!"

"Calm down, Robbie," said Bill Wirick. He

spoke coolly but firmly. "I had an easy play at second. It was obvious."

"Yeah? Well, it wasn't so obvious to me!"

"But it was to me," said Wire as calmly as before.

At this point, Coach Gus Franklin joined their huddle on the mound. "Good play, Wire," he said, patting his pitcher on the back.

Then Coach Franklin turned to Robbie and said, "I don't know what you were thinking about when you called for him to throw to first, Robbie. If Wire had thrown there, they'd have their tying run on second now with one of their best hitters up. Wake up!"

Robbie didn't say anything for a moment. He knew Coach Franklin was right.

"Sorry, Wire," said Robbie.

"No big deal, Robbie," said Wire with a smile. "I'll do what you call next time, okay? It's just that this time—"

"Enough talk already!" said Coach Franklin, cutting Wire off. "We have a game to win here. Let's try to finish it before the rain comes."

Both Robbie and Wire looked up. Dark clouds were drifting in fast from the east. A distant rumble of thunder could be heard.

"Now get on with it," barked Coach Franklin. "And *you*, Robbie, had better get your head into this game!" With that, Riverton's coach ran quickly from the mound.

Robbie hustled back to his position. He was

smarting from Coach Franklin's words. *He never talked like that to me before!*

Robbie felt shaken. As he gave Wire the signal for the next pitch, Robbie could feel his hand trembling. But when he rose to a half crouch to receive the pitch, a calm came over him. He knew the runner on first would steal on this pitch or the next. Robbie loved steal situations. He almost always threw out the runner. He had a quick release and a powerful, accurate arm. Melinda once timed his throw to second at 2.4 seconds.

But this steal situation had its problems. The runner was Willie Johnson, the Falcons' quick second baseman. The batter was left-handed, making Robbie's throw harder. And Wire's unusual pitching deliveries allowed the runner to take a big lead from first.

The batter was catcher Dale Davis, who batted third in the Hanover order. Robbie felt almost sure Davis would take the first pitch. Wire had been wild the last two innings. Davis would want the advantage of being ahead on the count. And he'd also be taking to give Willie Johnson a chance to steal. Robbie gave Wire a down-the-middle target and called for a fast ball.

Davis took the pitch for a called strike. The runner was tearing for second! Robbie caught the ball as he rose to a standing position. The ball was in his hand instantly. He stepped to his left to avoid Davis. Then Robbie cocked the ball and pegged it to Ty covering the bag. It was a perfect throw, except for one thing.

Willie Johnson beat it.

Robbie couldn't believe it. *Maybe Johnson is faster than I thought!*

More thunder rumbled through the darkening sky. Robbie heard Coach Franklin call to him, "C'mon, Robbie! Heads up in there!"

Robbie was shocked. *Coach is blaming me again! Why is he on my case?*

A big raindrop hit home plate with a splat. Then slow rain started to fall. A few fans opened umbrellas. Since the game had gone longer than five innings already, it would still count even if it was rained out. But so far, the rain wasn't heavy. Riverton and Hanover might yet get nine innings in.

Dale Davis was eager to bring in the tying run from second. Robbie knew that he hit fast balls well. But since it was getting dark and stormy, a fast ball might be harder to see. The rain might make the ball too slippery for Wire to throw a curve. So Robbie called for a fast ball.

It was a mistake.

Wire threw it well, but Davis stepped into it and sent it sailing. The ball lined deep into the opposite field. Robbie's heart sank. Dennis Wu, the Tiger left fielder, was running back as fast as he could. *No homer! Please, no homer!* Robbie prayed in his mind.

Suddenly, Dennis Wu slipped on the wet grass. But somehow he stayed on his feet and continued running. Dennis ran to the fence and crouched, ready to leap for the ball when it arrived. He didn't wait long. The small but agile left fielder jumped as high as he could. His legs spread out as he stuck his glove up. The ball smacked right into the pocket of his mitt!

It was a great catch. Willie Johnson had already rounded third. Now, he had to scramble like mad to get back to second. Dennis Wu came down from his jump with a jarring thud, but still held onto the ball. He threw it to second. The fleet Willie Johnson just beat the throw.

Plainly disappointed, Dale Davis trotted back to Hanover's bench. As he passed Robbie, he said, "Thanks for the fast ball, but not for the left fielder!"

A feeling of guilt swept over Robbie. He should never have called for another fast ball to Davis. Robbie sneaked a glance toward his own bench. Coach Franklin was staring at him. The coach knew every pitch Robbie called. And he knew that last one had been a turkey. Then the coach clapped his hands and called, "Forget it, Robbie! Two outs! Get this one!"

The light rain had now become steady rain. Almost all the fans were putting umbrellas or newspapers over their heads.

Wire stood on the mound, waiting. He looked as if he were wilting in the rain. The visor of his cap dripped water in front of his face. He wanted the game called—and now. Wire didn't want to pitch to Hanover's cleanup hitter, a burly right

18

fielder named Clarence Corkhill. So far, Wire had managed to keep Corkhill off the bases. But who knew how long that would last?

Corkhill's teammates on the bench began yelling out to the plate umpire. "He's stalling, ump!" "Make him pitch, ump!" "Delay of game!" "How long do we have to wait, ump?"

Finally, the plate umpire spoke. "Play ball!" he said to Wire.

The Riverton pitcher sighed and got down to business. Wire carefully worked Hanover's clean-up hitter to a 3–2 count. It seemed as if the rain fell harder with each pitch. Before throwing his next pitch, Wire asked, "What about it, umpire?" He was holding his hand out and gazing up at the rain. The base paths were dark brown now.

"Play ball!" ordered the umpire. "Now!"

Wire had no choice but to do as he was told. He looked in for Robbie's signal. In this tricky 3–2 situation, Robbie called for a safe fast ball. Wire delivered it with a rising hop. The batter swung up at it. The faint click of bat meeting ball was almost lost in the rushing sound of the rain. The ball shot straight up. It climbed higher and higher over Robbie's head.

Uh-oh, thought Robbie. He took off his mask and squinted up into the stinging rain. He couldn't find the ball and felt a moment of panic. But then he spotted a shadow of movement high in the air. It was the ball, looking like a dark gray pea against a slate background. It seemed to be just hanging there.

19

Robbie stood still. His face was turned up. His eyes were narrowed into slits, blinking and twitching. Water streamed from his face. He still held his iron catcher's mask in his right hand. He was waiting to see where the ball would come down. Then he'd toss the mask where it wouldn't trip him.

The ball now seemed to be growing bigger. *It's coming down!* thought Robbie. His body was leaning to the right. He let himself drift in that direction. He still couldn't tell exactly where the ball was going to come down. *Enough of this drifting!* he thought. He stopped and heaved the mask ten yards to his right.

The ball seemed to move in slow motion at the top of its flight. But it zoomed down for the last twenty yards. Robbie took a few steps backward. Then a few quicker steps backward. It was falling behind his head!

He ran backward as fast as he could. He put his catcher's mitt over his head. The ball fell into the mitt as Robbie fell onto the ground. But the ball never popped loose. "Out!" called the umpire. The inning was over.

Tiger fans clapped and cheered the catch as the rain began to pour. Puddles were already forming along the base paths. The Riverton players hurried off the field and into the shelter of the dugout.

"That should've been an easy catch, Robbie," Coach Franklin said to him as he passed by.

"Uh, the rain made it a little hard to see,

Coach," said Robbie. He was surprised at the remark.

"The rain? You blame the rain for that?" Coach Franklin was shaking his head. "You still have a lot of work to do, Robbie. A *lot* of work. Your concentration is muddier than that field out there!"

At that moment, lightning cracked the sky. Riverton and Hanover fans together went "Oooo!" Thunder boomed louder than ever, and the wind picked up speed. In sheets of rain, the plate umpire made the call everyone now expected. "Game called on account of—"

Thunder drowned out his last word. Soaked to the skin, the umpire stood his ground and yelled out once more, "Rain!" Then he dashed off the field.

The fans rushed from the stands toward the parking lot. Players and coaches from both teams quickly piled into the locker rooms. The Tigers had come away with a soggy 3–2 victory. Robbie had a key hit and two runs batted in. He should have been happy. But he wasn't. Instead, one thought stuck with him: *Why is Coach Franklin so down on me?*

Chapter Three

Monday was what Robbie and his teammates called "Room 307 Day." Room 307 was the high school's "Media Communications" classroom. Three communications courses were taught there. Other classes used it to watch educational films or videos. It was also used by the school newspaper and other school groups, including the athletic teams. It was where the baseball team watched video replays of its games while Coach Franklin commented.

The Monday after the Hanover game was Robbie's worst "Room 307 Day" ever.

In the darkened room, the team watched Melinda's videotape of the game on a large screen. Gus Franklin was in charge of the remote control. He liked to repeat a play many times or in slow motion to point out something.

The team cheered when Ty began the game with a single and two steals. But everyone grew

23

quiet as the coach replayed Abbie Jacobs's called third strike.

"Look at your bat, Abbie," Gus said. "There! It's still on your shoulder and the ball is halfway home!"

Dennis Wu squirmed in the seat next to Robbie. Dennis was the next batter on the large video screen.

"I missed this first pitch by a foot!" he whispered to Robbie.

On the screen, Dennis swung and missed.

"Nice swing, Dennis," the coach said. He meant it, too. "You only missed it by a hair. But why is everyone swinging at first pitches? That could easily have been called a ball."

Melinda Clark was sitting on the other side of Robbie. Sometimes in these sessions, Coach Franklin would have a comment for her, usually thanking her for a helpful shot. She also used the replay session to log some statistics for the team. As the coach took the team step by step through Dennis's strikeout, an unusual thing happened to Robbie.

Melinda was wearing a Tiger T-shirt. Her bare arm lightly grazed Robbie's bare arm as she jotted down figures on her stat sheets. The unusual thing was that Robbie enjoyed how it felt.

Then, thinking about Joshua Kenny, Robbie moved his arm away from Melinda's. *Easy, fellow,* he thought to himself. *Josh is a friend, and so is Melinda. Keep it that way.* Joshua Kenny used to be the equipment manager for Riverton's baseball team. Now he was away at Redstone University. Melinda and Josh had dated in high school, and they were still seeing each other as far as Robbie knew.

"Psst!"

Robbie blinked back to reality. Melinda was whispering to him now. "Better get ready." Her eyes flicked toward the screen. "Your turn."

"And here we have another first-pitch swinger," Coach Franklin's voice sang out. "The guy hasn't batted in two years! You'd think he'd want to take at least one pitch just to get the feel again. And you'd certainly think he'd look down at his coach for the sign! You'd also think he'd see the coach giving him the take sign! But no, this guy doesn't look at anything. But we'll forgive him! It's his first time up in a long time. He won't miss a sign again all year, will he, Robbie?"

"No, sir," Robbie mumbled.

The coach ran the clip of Robbie's foul tip over and over again. Robbie hadn't realized how awkward that swing had looked.

"The point about taking the first pitch is this," the coach went on. "If it's a bad pitch, you're ahead of the pitcher. If it's a good pitch, the pitcher will probably try it again, and you'll be ready!"

Robbie winced as the next pitch went by him for a strike. He was surprised when the coach said, "Actually Robbie, you were smart not to swing at this pitch, even though it was a called strike. It was the first time you saw his curve,

25

and it showed you something. You were too off balance to swing. Good take!"

Gus Franklin gave the strangest compliments sometimes. He also commended Robbie for taking the next two pitches, but not the third.

"I can't believe you took this one, Robbie!" he said in a loud voice. On the screen, Robbie and Hanover's catcher turned around to hear the umpire's delayed call of "ball." Robbie's heart raced again just watching it. His concentration *did* need work.

Coach Franklin thanked Melinda for her next action sequence of Ty Williams's walking lead off third. Then he told Ty he had gone too far in distracting Danny Stewart, the Falcon pitcher. "He waited you out, and Robbie's rhythm was broken in the batter's box. But you learned anyway. Your next lead was distracting just enough."

On the screen, Stewart pitched to Robbie, and Robbie stroked the ball crisply over the center fielder's head. His swing had none of the awkwardness of his first cut. It was smooth, strong, and confident.

Robbie didn't expect the coach to show his double again. But the coach was fair. He showed it a number of times.

"Gentlemen, and lady," Coach Franklin said, nodding toward Melinda, "take a good look at that swing. It's a beauty, nice and easy. Notice Robbie's eyes fixed on the ball. Notice his concentration. Do *you* notice it, Robbie?"

"Uh, yes, sir, I do." Robbie felt the weight of everyone's stare.

"Good," said the coach, pressing a button on the remote control in his hand. "Let's move on."

Melinda patted Robbie's knee. "That was a good hit, slugger. And you scored Ty." Pulling her hand back, she said, "Coach is in rare form today, huh?"

Robbie said nothing. He was watching the screen and listening to Coach Franklin's comments. The coach was pointing out every little catching mistake Robbie made—and there were many! He didn't like many of the pitches Robbie called for. He sharply criticized Robbie's next two at-bats, flies to the outfield. He said Robbie had been swinging too hard at bad pitches both times.

The videotape rolled on to the sixth inning. Robbie expected Coach Franklin to criticize Wire for losing control. But the coach was very mild with Wire. When Wire's wild pitch was shown, Coach Franklin lit into Robbie for not stopping it!

"I know it was scored as a wild pitch, Robbie. But I've seen you stop wilder pitches than that one!"

Robbie watched the screen. Wire's steep curve shot way outside into the dirt and took a crazy bounce. Robbie stuck his glove out. The ball skipped past it.

"You're just waving your glove at the ball, Robbie!" the coach said. "You should be throwing your whole body at the ball to stop it! Even Hanover's catcher, Dale . . . Dale . . ."

"Davis, Coach," said Sam Thorne reluctantly, sliding a bit lower in his chair. None of the players wanted to catch the coach's eye today.

"Right. Davis. Even *he* threw himself on that bad pitch against *you*, Robbie! And Eddie here"— the coach motioned toward Mosely now—"was all over bad pitches last year!"

"I still got the bruises to prove it, Coach!" Eddie cracked.

Robbie clenched his teeth. Watching Mosely squat behind the plate last year had been tough for Robbie to take. He leaned sideways and whispered, "Melinda, what was that passed ball stat you told me about?"

"You mean PBTRIR?" she whispered back. "Passed Balls That Resulted in Runs. Mosely had seven last year. You had twelve the year before. Coach is right, Rob. You could use some work on blocking wild pitches."

The session ground on. The team had been in Room 307 over an hour when the videotape reached the last inning before the game was called. Robbie dreaded what he knew was coming up.

Wire walked the first batter. Coach Franklin repeated what he had been saying to Wire about his control problem. "Every time you start losing your control, Wire, it's because you rush your delivery. Look at that! You start your wind-up smoothly, then all of a sudden you're racing through it! See what happens? Your arm gets stiff. No life in a stiff! Good thing it was a ball. If it had been a strike, the batter would've ripped it."

With the next batter, the whole team could see that Wire had slowed down his delivery. He threw a strike over the inside corner. Gus Franklin ran Wire's delivery over and over, complimenting his pitcher.

"Great recovery, Wire!"

"I remember telling myself to take more time in the wind-up," Wire said.

"And it worked! Just look at that. And good call, Robbie. That inside pitch really handcuffed the batter."

He's being nice now, thought Robbie, *but just wait ten seconds!*

The screen showed Wire fielding the weak hit, then whirling to throw the lead runner out at second. The coach ran the play backward, saying, "And now, gentlemen and lady, we have the worst play of the game." Robbie groaned out loud. His teammates laughed.

Gus Franklin froze the action just as Wire was picking up the ball. "This is where Robbie called for Wire to throw to first," he said.

"First?" Eddie Mosely piped up. "Why'd you call first, Robbie? Look at that lead runner!" At the top of the screen, the Falcon lead runner was only halfway to second.

Coach Franklin went on. "Look now, Robbie, because you sure didn't look during the play itself!" He let the action run. You could hear Robbie's call of "First!" weakly over the sound system. The room was dead quiet.

"Any other time, Wire, I'd burn your ears for ignoring the catcher's call here," said the coach, still annoyed. "Your back's to the lead runner, and you have to rely on the field judgment of a teammate here—in this case, the catcher." Coach Franklin looked at Robbie now. "But if your catcher is half-asleep out there, that's not your fault, but his!" The coach looked again at Wire. "You made the right decision, Wire. Good play! Nice to see *somebody* awake out there."

Robbie's cheeks were red with embarrassment. He looked down at his shoes.

The action on the screen continued. It showed Hanover's Willie Johnson sliding safely into second base with a steal.

"Here, our catcher gets stolen on," said Coach Franklin. "Not our pitcher. Wire's delivery is good. Our catcher looks as if he's moving underwater."

It was true. Robbie looked lazy as he caught the ball and threw it to second. No wonder Willie beat the throw.

"I'm making a list, Robbie, of things for you to work on," said the coach. "We'll add throwing to second base with a left-hander up."

The next pitch began, and Robbie felt like running from the room. This was the fast ball Dale Davis creamed. "And here's the pitch that could have lost our opening game. Robbie, you don't call for a fast ball down the middle against someone who's already hit one for RBIs! Luckily, we had a hero to save the day."

The team's mood brightened now. They all remembered Dennis Wu's fantastic catch. Robbie looked at Dennis. Dennis had a little smile of anticipation. *I'm glad someone is enjoying the show*, Robbie thought. On the screen, Riverton's left fielder slipped but kept his feet. The team, including Robbie, applauded his effort. "Great going, Dennis!" said the coach. "You came to play!"

Of all the remarks Coach Franklin had made during this grueling session, that last one stung Robbie the most. Robbie's favorite major-league star, Eddie Trent, had once autographed a ball for Robbie. Eddie Trent had written those exact words, "You came to play." *And Coach Franklin knows that!* Robbie thought. The New York Titans' all-star catcher was a friend of Coach Franklin's.

The team exploded into cheers and applause. On the screen, Dennis jumped and speared the ball just as it was about to fly over the fence. Grinning, Gus Franklin ran the leaping catch over and over. "Yes indeed," he concluded, "there's one player who came to play!"

Coach Franklin didn't have much to say as the next batter ran the count to 3–2 and the rain got heavier. Then the batter hit the high pop-up in the rain.

"Your concentration looked good up to here,

31

Robbie," said the coach. He was looking at the screen. "Then you stopped moving. Why? You're still not under the ball yet."

The videotape now showed Robbie backing up furiously. The team made a kind of rising groan as Robbie went after the falling ball. When he caught it and fell over, the team cheered.

That was the end of the game and the tape. The lights in the room were turned back on. The players blinked their eyes.

"Okay, into the locker room, suit up, and then out onto the field, folks," said Coach Franklin. "We'll get in an hour of practice today. We'll do a few concentration exercises, too! Okay! Hustle, hustle!"

The team moved quickly for the locker room.

"Does the coach seem to be picking on me more than the others?" Robbie asked Melinda once they were out of the room.

"Hmm, I guess so," Melinda said thoughtfully. "But that's not necessarily bad. Look, if he didn't care about you, do you think he'd bother at all?"

"Well, if he does care, he sure has a strange way of showing it," said Robbie, not entirely convinced.

"Everybody is different, Robbie. Coach has his way, you have yours, I have mine, and Josh has his."

"Josh? What made you bring up Josh?"

"Oh, I forgot to tell you. Josh is planning to come home next weekend. He said he wanted to see me. But I have a sneaking suspicion he

32

also wants to take in the game against Monsey."

Redstone University, which Josh Kenny now attended, was a hundred miles from Riverton. *Leave it to Josh to make the trip back during the weekend of the Monsey game*, thought Robbie. The Monsey Pirates always gave the Tigers a tough time on the field.

"Great!" said Robbie. "It'll be like old times again."

"Maybe," said Melinda. She had an odd look on her face. "A lot can happen in a year."

"Tell me about it," said Robbie. He held up the thumb he had broken and waggled it at her. "*Tell* me about it."

"You better get going, Robbie. Have a good practice."

"Thanks. See you, Melinda."

As Robbie opened the door to the locker room, he glanced back. Melinda hadn't moved an inch—and was staring straight at him.

Chapter Four

It was a rough week for Robbie. In all his life, he'd never worked so hard in baseball practice. He'd been very successful during his first two years of high-school ball. This tempted him to think he didn't have much more to learn about the sport. But Coach Franklin proved him wrong.

To strengthen Robbie's concentration, the coach pitted Robbie in one contest after another with Eddie Mosely at Tuesday's practice. He knew Robbie would rather die than let Mosely beat him at anything. This certainly made Robbie pay attention! And the drills were so hard, Robbie had to be on his toes every second.

By far the hardest drill was something Eddie Mosely called "bruise ball." The coach would stand halfway between home and the pitching rubber. From there, he would fire ball after ball at the catcher. Each one bounced nastily. The catcher had to do anything in his power to stop the ball from getting by.

Besides Robbie and Mosely, there was a third catcher on the team this year. He was a big but not yet very coordinated freshman named Guy Henry. Guy wasn't good at catching these bouncing balls cleanly. But he was better than Robbie or Mosely at just blocking them. Guy threw his big bulk at every short-hopper without fear. His two hundred pounds absorbed the shocks easily. Not one of the coach's skipping throws got past Guy.

Three got past Mosely; two got past Robbie. Robbie and Mosely ended up with colorful bruises, but Guy had none. Robbie had one on his forearm and one on the front of his thigh.

During a brief break in practice, Melinda gestured for Robbie to come over to where she was sitting. "Your PBTRIR should go down if you keep improving like that," she said.

"Whew! That's a relief!" said Robbie in mock seriousness. "It should also boost my MSOE."

"Your what?" Melinda riffled the stat sheets on her lap, searching for MSOE. Robbie gently grabbed her hand to stop her.

"MSOE. Much Stomped On Ego." Robbie winked and laughed.

"Very funny," said Melinda, a bit miffed. "Did it take you all week to come up with that?"

"Melinda, I was only kidding," said Robbie, still smiling. "Sometimes you take your alphabet soup of stats a little too seriously, you know."

"No, I don't know. If you took your stats as seriously as I do, they'd be a lot better."

35

"Okay, okay, you win," he said, heading back to home plate.

"The point isn't whether *I* win," she called after him, "but whether the *team* wins. Right?"

Without turning around, Robbie yelled "Right!"

"What's right, Robbie?" The question came from Coach Franklin. He was teaching Guy Henry something.

"Oh, nothing, Coach."

"You're telling me," he said sternly. "Give Guy here a hand."

When Robbie taught Guy something, it made Robbie feel he himself had finally learned it for good. It reminded Robbie of when he had learned how to catch as a freshman. Robbie had been taught by a tough but friendly senior named Mojo Johnson. Robbie was doing with Guy what Mojo had done with Robbie. It was like passing on a tradition.

Guy learned well. Since the sixth grade, he had been a fan of Robbie's. So he hung on Robbie's every word. Guy tried his best to do whatever Robbie suggested. He was willing to make mistakes in order to learn. Guy had grown a lot recently, and his new size made him awkward. But he had a strong throwing arm, great hustle, and good power as a hitter.

Coach Franklin next went into a concentration exercise for the whole team. Robbie found this the hardest drill of all. The coach told the whole team to face him, stand still, and not move for a minute. It was the longest minute of the practice. Even the hard-blowing calisthenics and sprints the team did at the beginning of each practice would have been better than this.

While they were all standing as still as statues, Coach Franklin would hold up a new ball. "Eye on the ball!" he'd say. Then he'd slowly move the ball around. The players had to follow it with their eyes. If a player's mind started to wander, his eyes stopped tracking the ball. The coach could see this instantly. He would call the person's name, getting his eyes back on the ball.

Robbie was amazed how often the coach would call his name. It seemed like such an easy thing to do—stand still and watch the ball. But he would start daydreaming about all sorts of things.

He thought of the strange look Melinda gave him before he entered the locker room yesterday. Then he thought about seeing Josh Kenny this weekend. Robbie hadn't seen Josh since he left for college.

"Robbie?" The coach caught him looking off the ball.

"Sorry, Coach." Robbie fixed his eyes on the ball.

But then another thought intruded. He worried about his father and the eye trouble he'd been having. The eye doctor had found a problem in Simon's left eye. Its main nerve, called the "optic nerve," was swollen. This was called "optic neuritis." It could be caused by any number of things. The eye doctor wasn't sure what yet. More tests had to be done. Meanwhile, Simon's vision was still blurred. It was getting a little better, but not much.

Robbie remembered getting out of bed very late one night to get a drink of juice in the kitchen. As he passed the living room, Robbie saw his father. He was sitting in a recliner with a Walkman on. When Robbie opened the refrigerator door, the light caught his father's attention.

"Thirsty, Rob?" Simon Belmont called out.

"Yeah, Dad. Want some juice?"

"Don't mind if I do."

St. Simon Belmont came into the kitchen and sat by the table. Robbie poured juice into two glasses and gave one to his father.

"Thanks," said Simon, taking a sip.

"Listening to music, Dad?"

"Oh, no. Reading." Simon saw the puzzled look on his son's face. "Books on cassettes. It's the only way I can read now. I just pop in the cassette, put the earphones on, and listen."

"What are you listening to, er, reading now?"

"Your favorite—Shakespeare," said Simon, chuckling.

Robbie groaned.

"You ought to try it, Rob." Simon's smile suddenly faded. "Something new is happening. When I move my eyes in the dark, I see a bright flash. It's weird, and I don't like it. I'll have to mention it to the eye doctor."

Robbie was thinking of his father sitting there and seeing flashes in the dark. That's when Coach Franklin's voice boomed out. "Robbie? Robbie!"

Robbie snapped to and started watching the ball again. It was not always easy to concentrate. Coach Franklin said it was normal to get distractions. What he wanted them to learn was how to get through them.

On Wednesday, it rained. The team practiced inside the school gym. An hour into the practice, Gus Franklin called the three catchers over. He was holding the special long, thin bat called a fungo bat. He pushed open one of the metal exit doors that led outside and said, "After you, gentlemen!" They all trudged through the drizzle to the soggy outfield. Then Coach Franklin began hitting them high pop-ups!

Robbie caught the first five. But he barely got to the first three, lunging at the last moment. "It's not the rain that keeps you from catching it. It's your concentration!" said the coach. He fungoed another one high into the air.

The rain doesn't help any! Robbie thought to himself. He felt miserable. As he squinted up into the drizzle, he heard Gus Franklin talking quietly to him. "Let yourself drift, Robbie. That's it. Keep loose. Relaxed concentration is the key. Keep your eyes on the ball and let your body lead. That's it! That's it!"

And the ball came down perfectly into Robbie's mitt! There was no last-second lunge or panic this time. Gus hit him one more pop-up. Robbie actually enjoyed gazing up after it. He settled under it for another easy catch.

"Way to go," said the coach. He and Robbie

exchanged smiles. Finally, Robbie had caught on to what the coach had been talking about.

Eddie Mosely and Guy Henry had a lot more trouble with the pop-ups. The more the coach told Mosely to relax, the stiffer Mosely would get. "They seem like opposites, Coach," Mosely said. "You're either relaxing or you're concentrating. How can you do both?"

Guy Henry was determined he was going to catch a pop-up in the rain. He staggered around in circles for a while. Doggedly, he kept staring up, searching for the ball. When he finally saw it, he ran as hard as he could about ten yards to the right. The ball came down exactly where he had been before he ran away!

"I guess you worked *too* hard for that one, son," Coach Franklin told Guy.

By the fifth try, Guy was no longer looking like a crazed Frankenstein monster when he went after the pop-up. He caught it—his first one! It wasn't a smooth catch, but it wasn't a lucky stab either.

The coach hit pop-ups for fifteen more minutes. Robbie marveled at how well Gus Franklin hit this unusual fly ball. The coach had to swing his fungo bat almost straight up in the air. But the thin bat socked the wet ball dead center almost every time.

Coach Franklin asked Guy and Eddie to go back inside. "Tell the team to run twenty laps and call it quits," he told Eddie.

When they were gone, the coach hit Robbie

another pop-up. This one was much higher than before. Robbie stood there looking up. "I think that one's in orbit, Coach," he said.

Coach Franklin laughed. Robbie finally caught a glimpse of the ball coming down. He drifted five yards on a diagonal. Then he trotted two more and put his glove in front of his stomach. The ball plopped into it with a wet smack. Robbie grinned and tossed it to the coach, saying, "This is fun!"

"That's what it's mainly about, Robbie."

The coach hit some towering pop-ups to Robbie for ten more minutes. Toward the end, he hit another ball right after hitting the first. This put two balls in the air at the same time! At first, Robbie missed both of them. The second time, he caught one. He caught both the third time. Then Coach Franklin started hitting *three* balls into the air, one right after the other.

It took Robbie about five minutes to reach the point where he could even lay a glove on all three balls falling. Five minutes after that, he was catching all three balls falling.

"That's a good way to end," said the coach.

Before opening one of the metal doors to go back inside, Coach Franklin stopped. He waved his hand toward the diamond and said, "Look, Robbie."

"I see what you mean about not blaming the rain, Coach," Robbie said.

It had only been drizzling when they started their pop-up practice. Now, it was pouring.

Thursday and Friday, practice was held outside in the sunshine. Coach Franklin was really pushing his team. Robbie couldn't remember the last time the Tigers held practice every day of the week. The Monsey game scheduled for Saturday was on everybody's mind.

The stands on both sides of Riverton's home field were jammed on Saturday afternoon. The rivalry between the two teams was a long, intense one. Faces not seen at other Riverton home games would be seen at Monsey games. People were standing alongside the bleachers—that's how crowded it was!

Joshua Kenny came early enough to watch the Tigers take batting practice before the game. He was smiling and greeting team members. Even Coach Franklin walked over and shook Josh's hand, welcoming him back. Josh had been an unofficial assistant to the coach as well as Riverton's equipment manager during his high-school years.

"Yo, Robbie!" shouted Josh with a smile to Robbie, standing in the batting cage. "Knock one out for me!"

Next pitch in, Robbie swung and clouted it over the left-field fence. "How's that?"

"Great!" said Josh. "Now do it in the game. I didn't travel a hundred miles to watch Riverton lose, you know."

Josh moved to where Melinda was sitting in the first row of the bleachers. Born with an inability to straighten his legs, Josh walked with some difficulty. Yet he never complained. Robbie recalled a fan once coming up to Josh and saying, "I'm so sorry about your handicap." Josh replied without hesitation: "Why? I'm not."

Eagle Wilson was also here today. He had been the Tigers' star pitcher when Robbie was a freshman catcher. Now, he was one of Redstone University's starting pitchers. He sat behind Joshua and Melinda. Sitting quietly next to Eagle was Cynthia Wu.

Cynthia was Dennis Wu's older sister. Robbie had met Cynthia his freshman year, when she helped him find a baseball book in the library. Robbie's stomach would knot every time he saw her. He thought she was beautiful, inside and out. Robbie knew she had been going out with Eagle Wilson, off and on, for three years. Dennis Wu kept Robbie informed how Eagle and Cynthia were getting along.

The news Robbie most liked hearing was that they were not getting along. Eagle and Cynthia had split up and gotten back together many times in three years. Cynthia usually got more interested in Robbie when she was on the outs with Eagle.

Last year, Eagle was away at college and Cynthia was still at Riverton High School. Robbie wasn't playing baseball because of his injury, so he had a lot of extra time. When Cynthia and Eagle broke up again, he was ready. He made a point of talking with her more. Soon, they were spending some time with each other almost every day. All went well for two weeks. Then Eagle began calling Cynthia on the phone again. Cynthia still hung out with Robbie. But sometimes she would talk about Eagle. It wasn't Robbie's favorite topic, though he knew Cynthia needed to talk about Eagle.

Then one day, while eating lunch, Cynthia said to Robbie, "I've asked Eagle to the senior prom." She tried to explain. She said something about how much Eagle wanted to see the high school again.

Robbie nodded politely, but didn't hear much. He was stunned. He and his teammates sometimes made fun of the senior prom. But still, it meant something to Robbie. This was especially true of Cynthia's senior prom. He secretly hoped she'd ask him to go with her. But that hope was gone now. *Guess she wants to impress her friends by going out with a college guy instead of a high-school junior like me!* he thought.

Robbie had gobbled his lunch and left quickly. After that, he didn't hang out with Cynthia much. He gave up on the idea of asking her out again. The sight of her still gave him a rush of excitement when their paths crossed. And they were still on speaking terms. Cynthia knew a lot about baseball, and Robbie liked talking with her about it.

Then, Cynthia had graduated and gone to Redstone. She was still dating Eagle. They still kept breaking up and getting back together.

Robbie had only seen her twice since she went away. He still thought about her many times during the course of a day. But he had been doing that so long, it seemed ordinary to him.

Robbie often talked about his feelings for Cynthia with his best friend, Brian Webster. Brian was Coach Franklin's unofficial assistant this year.

On occasion, Robbie also talked about Cynthia with Melinda. Melinda knew all about how he felt for Cynthia. But lately, Melinda would frown every time he brought the subject up.

The pregame warm-ups continued, and Robbie and Brian had a chance to talk. "Do you think we should go over and say hello to the gang sitting around Melinda?" Robbie asked.

"It would look funny if we didn't," said Brian.

"Cynthia looks great," said Robbie.

"Steady as she goes, buddy," said Brian.

The two walked over to their friends. After the hello's and how-are-you's, there was an awkward silence.

Then Robbie said, "So, Josh, what's it like being an assistant to a college coach?"

"It's a lot easier," the pleasant, curly-headed Joshua replied. "For one thing, you don't have to deal with any high-school players!"

Robbie laughed. Joshua went on. "No, actually, it *is* easier. Everything's so organized. But I miss you guys and Coach Franklin, and Melinda especially," he finished.

"Mmm," nodded Robbie. He saw Cynthia and Melinda both give him a hard look as he started to say something. This made him decide to say nothing.

"How's this pitcher for Monsey?" Eagle asked. Eagle seemed uninterested in anything but the players on the field. His blond hair looked even blonder in the early spring sunshine. There was an elastic bandage wrapped around his left wrist. It seemed that Eagle always wore a bandage somewhere on his body.

"Russ Thurmon is his name," said Melinda. "He's a smart pitcher. Throws a lot of off-speed pitches."

"I've been throwing more off-speed pitches lately," said Eagle, looking thoughtfully into the sky.

"Why do you always turn every remark into something about yourself?" asked Cynthia.

"Would you mind not bawling me out in public?" Eagle said to her sharply.

Robbie hated hearing anyone talk to Cynthia in that tone of voice. But Cynthia's remark had been cutting—even if it was true.

Melinda saw the troubled look in Robbie's eyes. "Good day for a game, Robbie!" she said.

Robbie was glad for the change of subject. He gave Melinda a big smile. Then he quickly frowned. He didn't want Joshua or Cynthia to think he liked Melinda too much. He looked around. Joshua and Cynthia were both looking at him strangely.

Robbie's head was spinning with confusion. He looked further up in the stands and saw his mother sitting alone. He waved and she waved back, a little sadly. A friend was staying with Simon at home today.

The medicine Robbie's father was now taking for his eye problem was steroids. All Robbie knew about them was to stay away from them. Coach Franklin had warned his team about any and all drugs at the start of the season. And he had mentioned steroids specifically. Knowing his father was now taking them under a doctor's supervision didn't make Robbie worry less about him.

"Come on, Rob. We'd better get back to the bench," Brian said.

"Yeah. Nice seeing you all," said Robbie. "Maybe we'll hook up after the game."

They all agreed. *Not too enthusiastically*, Robbie thought.

He walked back to the bench with Brian. The whole time, Robbie wondered how he was going to keep his mind on the game today.

Chapter Five

Russ Thurmon, Monsey's pitcher, had gotten bigger and meaner since Robbie last played against him. The Pirate hurler stood on the mound and glared at Robbie. The ball in Thurmon's hand looked like an aspirin in the paw of a bear.

Robbie hit a nice, clean single against Thurmon his first time up. Robbie's mind had been buzzing, but his eyes kept returning to the ball. Coach Franklin's concentration exercise was paying off.

Now, Robbie was up against Thurmon for the second time. The Riverton Tigers were ahead, 1–0, in the bottom of the fourth inning.

Russ Thurmon remembered Robbie had hit a fast ball for a single. He threw him three straight breaking pitches, making the count 2–1. Robbie guessed the fourth throw would be a curve. Instead, it was a zooming fast ball. Robbie swung late. But the weightlifting he did last year when he didn't play had made his arms powerful. Robbie still got good wood on the ball.

Whack! The shock of ball meeting bat was pure pleasure! Robbie tore for first base. The ball climbed deep between the right and center fielders. The home crowd got louder as the ball went deeper. It finally hit the base of the fence.

Robbie rounded second base and kept going. As he raced closer to third, he saw Coach Franklin waving for him to keep going. *An inside-the-park homer?* thought Robbie.

His right foot stomped the inside corner of the third-base bag. He raced toward home. The Pirates' catcher waited in front of the plate. Robbie launched into a hook slide. He slid past the catcher's leg, then past the plate. He still hadn't touched home!

Robbie clawed his way back to the plate. Monsey's catcher caught the bouncing throw. Robbie's fingers finally scratched onto the plate. The catcher's mitt tagged Robbie's head right after his hand touched home.

"You're out!" shouted the umpire.

"No way!" called Robbie, jumping up. "I touched home before he tagged me!"

"Out by a mile!" the umpire said loudly.

Robbie stood there speechless. "Out by a mile?" he finally said. The umpire pointed grandly to the Tigers' bench.

Shaking his head, Robbie trotted back to the Riverton bench. Tiger fans were jeering and booing the call. Robbie plopped down angrily on the bench.

"Tough break, Robbie! You were safe by a mile!" Brian said.

"Safe by a split second, anyway," Robbie grumbled. "What is it with that guy, anyway?"

The plate umpire had made a number of questionable calls since the game began. But calling Robbie out at home had been the first call to affect the score. It was still 1–0 in favor of Riverton.

Russ Thurmon retired the rest of the Tiger batters that inning with no further trouble. Robbie walked toward his catcher's position. Coach Franklin stopped him. "You got a bad call there, Robbie. Shake it off."

Robbie nodded and moved to his place behind the plate. The umpire stood watching five yards away. Right before the last warm-up pitch, Robbie called, "Second!" Robbie caught Wire's toss and pegged it furiously to second. Usually, he only threw at three-quarter speed to second on this practice throw. The slower speed might make the opponents think his arm was weaker than it was. But his silent anger at the umpire made this practice peg a sizzler. There was a loud *pock* when Tiger shortstop Ty Williams caught it.

As Robbie walked behind the plate, the umpire held out his catcher's mask.

"Thanks," Robbie muttered, taking it. *Keep cool*, he told himself between clenched teeth.

On Wire's first pitch, the Pirate batter squared

50

off to bunt. He stabbed at the ball with his bat. Wire's hopping fast ball rose past untouched.

"Ball one," said the umpire.

Robbie's jaw dropped. He didn't turn around, but said, "Ump, the batter poked his bat at it."

"Nope," said the umpire. "Play ball."

Robbie was still holding the ball. He stood there without moving for a few seconds.

"Play ball, sonny," the umpire said in a stern voice.

Robbie threw the ball back to Wire. There had been a few loud groans from other Tigers. Coach Franklin called out, "Never mind, Robbie! Easy batter! Easy batter!"

The batter squared away to bunt on the next pitch, a curve. The batter jumped back as the ball swooshed inside. He made no attempt to bunt it this time. But the ball curved over the plate beautifully at the last second.

"Ball two," said the umpire.

"What?" Robbie yelled, despite his efforts to remain cool. The entire Tiger bench screamed in protest. Riverton fans roared their disapproval. Coach Franklin trotted out a few steps and called, "Looked good, ump! Looked mighty good!"

The umpire whipped off his mask and screamed at Coach Franklin, "Sit down, Mr. Franklin, right now, or you're out of the game!"

Coach Franklin sat down, shaking his head.

No one was surprised when the umpire finally called ball four on the batter. The two other balls both looked like corner strikes to Robbie.

With each bad call, Robbie grew more frustrated and angry. Bill Wirick looked as if he'd been kicked in the teeth. He was throwing as well as he could, and that made it tougher to accept the plate umpire's calls.

"Don't worry about it, Wire," Robbie called out to his pitcher. "This batter's ours."

Wire nodded, then went into his stretch. Holding the runner at first base with a quick look, he unleashed a wicked fast ball that passed over the inside corner.

"Ball!" the plate umpire shouted.

Robbie nearly bit his tongue on that call. But he said nothing. Wire's next pitch clipped the outside corner of the plate.

"Ball two!" said the plate umpire.

"What can I do?" Robbie muttered under his breath.

"What's that you say, sonny?" asked the umpire.

"Could I have a time-out?" Robbie asked.

"Certainly," said the umpire. "Time!" he called, enjoying the booming sound of his voice.

Robbie walked to the mound. He looked over at Coach Franklin. The coach came out to the mound, too.

"What can we do, Coach?" Robbie asked. "Wire's been knocking in these great pitches. It seems like the umpire is making bad calls on purpose."

"Maybe concentration is the key to this problem, too," said the coach with a sly look.

"We've *been* concentrating," said Wire, "but it doesn't do any good with this ump."

"It's not only how well you pay attention," said Coach Franklin, "it's also what you pay attention *to*! Try this. Don't give him any attention when he makes bad calls. But when he makes a good call—"

"If he ever does," said Wire.

"If he ever makes a good call, *then* give him attention."

"Let's hurry it up, boys," said the umpire.

The "boys"—including Coach Franklin—all looked away from the umpire. Coach Franklin walked back to the bench. Wire looked down and poked the dirt in front of the pitching rubber with his foot. Robbie jogged back behind the plate.

The umpire was left standing with his nose lifted in the air between plate and mound. All the players were in position, waiting for *him*. He didn't seem to mind. He strolled slowly back to his position. Then he made a big deal of putting his mask back on. Finally, like a ringmaster in a circus, he called "Play ball!"

He comes out to speed things up, thought Robbie, *and he ends up slowing things down!*

Wire's first pitch was a fast ball straight down the middle of the plate. "Ball!" said the umpire.

Wire almost completely lost his cool. He stormed toward the plate. The umpire whipped off his mask and stomped out to meet Wire. The two marched toward each other. Robbie, however, could see Wire's face soften as he approached the umpire. The umpire halted as Wire came close.

"Listen, pitcher, if you think I'm going to put up with someone second-guessing my calls, you—" The umpire stopped talking when Wire walked right by him toward Robbie.

The slow breath Wire let out told Robbie how close Wire had come to sounding off. The Tiger pitcher was now trying to make it look as if he wanted to talk to his catcher all along.

"Say, Rob, could you give me a better target?" Wire winked as he said this.

"Sure, Wire. I don't know what got into me."

"Me neither," whispered Wire.

"Mind if we play some ball now, fellows?" said the plate umpire. He had calmed down, too.

"Yes, sir," Robbie and Wire said in unison. Wire headed back to the mound, Robbie dropped into his catcher's squat, and the umpire hunched behind him.

Wire's next pitch again split the middle. "Steeee-rike!" the umpire shouted, throwing his right hand into the air and running a few steps to the right. *You'd think he was the one responsible for the pitch!* thought Robbie. *What a ham!* Then he remembered Coach Franklin's advice: Give this umpire attention on the good calls. *This is going to be one of the hardest things I've ever done in baseball!* thought Robbie, gritting his teeth.

The plate umpire was returning to his position behind Robbie. "Good call, ump," said Robbie. The eyes behind the umpire's mask seemed to get bigger as they looked with thanks at Robbie. *Seems easy to convince*, thought Robbie. The Tiger bench was also calling out positive things toward the umpire. Coach Franklin must have spread the word.

"Good eye there, ump!"

"Nice call! Nice call!"

"Way to look in there, ump!"

Even Wire was getting in on the act. He stood on the mound and bobbed his head in agreement with the call.

The Tiger fielders didn't know what was going on. Robbie saw Ty Williams give a puzzled look to second baseman Todd Murphy, who shrugged. The fielders had not yet caught on to Coach Franklin's strategy.

With a count of three balls and one strike, the Pirate batter took Wire's next pitch. He was obviously hoping for a walk. To Robbie, the pitch looked like it just missed the outside corner.

"Steeeeerike twooooooo!" the umpire drawled. This time, he ran almost halfway down the first-base line. *Figures*, thought Robbie. *He likes bringing the count to 3–2. It makes his next call more important. This guy should be on a stage, not on a ball field.*

The Riverton bench and Wire again showed their approval for the call. They didn't overdo it, but Robbie was still amused.

Wire's next pitch was a curve ball that the

Pirate batter chopped hard to the mound. The ball bounced once, and Wire had to jump to catch it. As he did, Robbie had to make a split-second decision.

"Second base, Wire!" he shouted.

Wire heard the urgency in Robbie's voice. With his feet back on the ground, Wire whirled and fired the ball to Todd Murphy. The Tiger second baseman touched the bag, leapt up over the sliding Pirate runner, and sidearmed the ball to first base. Eddie Mosely, who remained in the starting line-up as a first baseman for Riverton, stretched out as far as he could. The ball came into his glove just before the batter's foot touched the bag. Double play!

The Tigers were charged up after that. The next Monsey batter went down on three straight swing-and-miss strikes. Riverton then scored five runs in the bottom of the fifth inning. Robbie and Eddie Mosely both hit home runs. Eddie Mosely had been working out with weights ever since his sophomore year. Now, as a senior, he had a weight lifter's build. He bulged with muscles. The extra bulk had slowed him down, but it had given him more power at the plate.

The plate umpire made a few more questionable calls, but they didn't bother the Tigers now. Robbie and Wire continued to approve the umpire's good calls and ignore his others. At times, the umpire even made some bad calls in favor of the Tigers.

Wire had a shutout going into the top of the

ninth inning. But Monsey, a never-say-die team, rallied for three runs. Two were unearned, as Tiger right fielder Abbie Jacobs misplayed a line drive that scored a pair of runs. The other run came when Wire hung a curve ball, which was clouted over the left-field fence for a homer. The Pirates managed to sprinkle a couple more hits, but they couldn't push any more runs across. The final score was 6–3.

Wire had pitched well, giving up a total of four hits and two walks. Ty Williams had gotten on base five straight times. Robbie hit a vicious double in the eighth inning, giving him three hits in five at-bats for the game. Though he was tagged out in the first inning when he tried for an inside-the-park homer, the hit was still scored as a triple. Robbie also threw out two Pirate runners trying to steal, and he blocked three possible wild pitches.

After the game, Coach Franklin told Robbie, "You played well. But there's still a number of things you need to work on. Your concentration is improving, but it still could be better."

In the locker room, Robbie was happy about the game but uneasy about seeing his friends afterward. Melinda would be with Joshua, and Cynthia would be with Eagle.

Would Melinda still act oddly toward Robbie with Joshua around? Would Cynthia treat him as no more than an old high-school acquaintance?

Robbie thought about how the Tigers had dealt with the plate umpire. Attention was a powerful thing, if used right. If he gave his attention to the right thing at the right time, he could get through anything.

Dressed in his best, Robbie strode out of the locker room, ready to turn his attention to his friends.

Chapter Six

Swanee's was the place Robbie and Brian headed to after the game. It had bad lighting, cracked vinyl seats with foam rubber sticking out, windows that hadn't seen a sponge in months, not enough menus, tiny bathrooms, and crabby waiters. But it also had good, cheap food—pizza in particular—and a great jukebox. As usual, the place was mobbed with Riverton High School students.

Robbie and Brian arrived ahead of their friends and found a table for six in the back. The two cleared from the table the soda cups and cardboard plates with pizza crusts still on them, then sat down. A couple of minutes later, Eagle, Cynthia, Josh, and Melinda came in.

"Back here!" shouted Brian, standing and waving.

The four slithered through the crush of students to get to the back. Robbie and Brian sat on opposite ends of the table, leaving the two chairs on either side of it open. Eagle and Cynthia sat in one pair of chairs, and Josh and Melinda sat in the other pair.

"Pizza, gang?" asked Brian, grabbing the lone menu.

Everyone else nodded.

"Go for the works?" he asked.

"Everything but anchovies," said Eagle. "They give me gas."

Cynthia looked at Eagle as if she couldn't quite believe her ears.

"You convinced me, Eagle," said Brian, closing the menu. "No fish on our pizza. Now the fun part begins—trying to flag a waiter."

Finally, they got one, who grunted as he took the order. When the waiter left, the six caught up on each other's news. Eventually, the conversation swung around to former Tiger players.

Tug Peters had been a second-string catcher three years ago and a starting first baseman two years ago for Riverton. Now in college, Tug still played baseball. But his main sport was football! He had turned his plumpness into muscle, and he had made all-conference first-string tackle the past winter.

John Roberts and Marty Walton both went to Fuller University, where Robbie's father taught English. Robbie told the group that John now played shortstop instead of third base. Marty played second, as he had for the Tigers. John and Marty had become a good double-play combination at Fuller, said Robbie.

Jim Nelson was now a sophomore at a West Coast college. The former Riverton right fielder had played college baseball as a freshman, but had not done well. He became active in student government and wasn't playing this year.

Earl Markley, a Tiger relief pitcher two years ago, was now a sophomore relief pitcher for Denton University. A teammate there was Leon Tucker, the slugger Robbie had a hitting duel with in the state championship game Riverton won two years back.

The table conversation stopped briefly when the jukebox music changed from pop to hard rock. Leaning over the jukebox by the door were Ralph Butler, Dennis Wu, and Patty Sanchez, Dennis's girlfriend. Ralph was wearing a big smile as a song by the band Axle Grease came out of the speakers.

Cynthia stood up from her chair and gestured for the three to come to the back table. As Ralph, Dennis, and Patty made their way, Robbie and Brian found three folding chairs tucked by the rear exit door. They opened them and placed them around the table.

"Hey, hey, hey!" said Ralph, greeting everyone at the table. "We thought you might be at Swanee's. Had to change the tunes, though. You know, they've found that listening to all that sweet soda pop music can give you pimples."

"I like pop music," said Cynthia.

"Me, too," said Melinda.

Ralph looked at them as if they had lost their

61

minds. "Just goes to show you that two wrongs never make a right. Ahem." He grinned as he sat down, and the two girls just winked at each other.

Before sitting down, Dennis Wu pulled a rolled magazine from his back pants pocket. "Guess what?" he said, holding up the magazine. "The new *Fisk & Foster* baseball issue!"

"All right!" said Brian, taking the magazine from Dennis and opening it. Every year around the start of baseball season, *Fisk & Foster* came out with a special edition on pro, college, and high-school teams and players. The rankings it gave were read by a lot of pro scouts and college coaches.

After his freshman season, Robbie Belmont was ranked among the top five high-school players in his state by *Fisk & Foster*. After his sophomore season, the year Riverton won the state title, *Fisk & Foster* ranked him first in his state and a second-team All-American. But Robbie missed all of last year's baseball season. Did the long layoff and thumb injury hurt his ranking?

The gang leaned forward as Brian spoke again. "Okay, here it is—top fifty high-school prospects. And this year's number two catching prospect in the nation is—ta da—Robbie Belmont!"

Robbie breathed out in relief as everyone but Eagle clapped and cheered.

"So who's the number one catching prospect?" Josh Kenny asked.

"A guy named Jason Jackson out of Chickaw, Oklahoma."

62

"Well, *Fisk & Foster* has been wrong before, and it's wrong now," said Melinda. "*We* know who's really number one." She turned and looked at Robbie, who blushed.

"It says here that Jason Jackson is also the number one high-school baseball prospect in the country at any position," added Brian.

"What's Robbie?" asked Melinda.

"Number ten overall!"

Everyone but Eagle clapped again. Robbie stood up and took a mock bow. He was happy with the ranking. But he also remembered what Coach Franklin once told him: "No one ever won a ball game with newsprint, Robbie. Rankings are fine, but it's what you do out on the field that counts."

Robbie really enjoyed seeing Josh again. Josh said he liked Redstone University. His major was architecture, and he had found a few teachers who really inspired him.

"I miss Melinda, though," he whispered to Robbie.

Robbie nodded in understanding. "She misses you, too, Josh. We all do. But what the heck—here you are."

"It's not that simple, Robbie." Joshua looked up and sighed.

The others were now talking in small groups. Eagle and Cynthia and Brian were talking. So were Dennis Wu and his girlfriend, Patty Sanchez. Patty was the younger sister of José Sanchez. José had been the Tigers' power-hitting center fielder during Robbie's first two years in high school. José was now playing baseball for a college in the Midwest. Patty said he led his team in extra-base hits last year.

Melinda Clark was talking with Ralph Butler, an Olympic track hopeful. The hard-working senior was a close friend of Robbie's.

"No, it's not that simple," Joshua repeated after a pause. "I went out on a few dates with another architecture major named Dori," Joshua said quietly. He was looking at Melinda to make sure she couldn't overhear. "I told Melinda about the dates. Funny thing is, she didn't get mad. She said it was okay to date others. Now I'm worried she's going to date someone else! Maybe I should stop seeing Dori so Melinda won't date anyone else. But Dori is, well, interesting. It's more a friendship than anything else. I don't know. It isn't that simple. Nothing is anymore. But other than that, I'm doing fine."

"Other than what?" said Melinda. She had finished talking with Ralph and was leaning toward Josh.

"Oh, nothing," said Joshua.

Melinda looked at Joshua, then at Robbie. She looked skeptical.

Suddenly, Eagle turned to them and asked, "So, Melinda, are you going to Redstone University, too?"

Another hot topic of the evening was where everyone was going to college next year. Still, Eagle's timing could have been better. Melinda hadn't decided where she was going yet. This caused some tension between her and Joshua, who wanted her to go to Redstone.

"Whoops, I must have touched a sore spot," said Eagle, laughing a little. Robbie saw Cynthia frown when Eagle laughed.

"Well, Eagle, actually I haven't decided yet," Melinda said. "Redstone is one of two places I'm considering. The other is Whalen University. Their computer science program is a really good one. On the other hand, Redstone has Josh. That's a big plus. On the other hand—"

"You just ran out of hands," said Joshua. "You're on your third hand."

"On the other *foot*," Melinda went on, smiling, "Whalen is more expensive. On the other . . . whatever, my parents say they can afford it. 'We'll just have to give up a few things,' my father says, 'like clothes and food.'"

"I think you should go to Whalen," said Joshua. Melinda looked at him in surprise. "I *do*," he said, "Don't look at me like that. You go to college to learn what you most want to learn. And that's what Whalen has for you. Your eyes light up when you talk about the computer courses Whalen has. All Redstone has is me—a truly wonderful guy, of course. But you could have both by going to Whalen."

"Hmm, you have a point there, Josh," said Melinda, looking at him fondly.

"What's the campus like at Whalen?" asked Robbie.

65

"Green hills," said Melinda. "Nice-looking buildings for class. Good-sized dorms. Big city fifteen minutes away."

"One thing I don't like about Redstone," Robbie said, "is that it's too far away from any interesting city."

"But as far as baseball goes," said Eagle, "it's one of the best colleges in the country. You don't get many managers better than Frank Preston."

Brian chimed in, "And Frank Preston is close friends with Mack Doogan, the main scout for the New York Titans."

"I know," said Robbie. "Coach Franklin knows Doogan, too. In fact, I'm supposed to meet Doogan sometime later in the season. If I have a good season—"

"No reason why you shouldn't!" cut in Melinda.

"Well, if I do," said Robbie, "Coach said he'll arrange a meeting with Doogan."

"The Titans have taken five players from Redstone in the last seven years!" said Brian. Brian very definitely planned to attend Redstone.

"I like Redstone's baseball program," Robbie said. "I also like the idea that so many of my friends are there and that it's not too far from home. But sometimes I think I should go to some entirely new place, someplace far away. Right now, I'm leaning toward Lansley University."

"But that's so far away!" Cynthia exclaimed. Her hand went to her mouth right after she said it.

Robbie looked at her. *Does Cynthia want me to go to Redstone, too?* he wondered.

"Some say Lansley is *the* university for baseball, though," said Eagle.

"If that's so," said Brian, "then why are you at Redstone?" Eagle had nothing to say to that. Brian continued. "Look, the Titans have not taken a player from Lansley in years. Most of Lansley's stars wind up in the other league."

"Well, it's a little too early to make decisions based on what major league I'll end up in!" said Robbie, laughing. Only Eagle laughed along with him. The others just looked at him curiously.

"It doesn't seem too early for that, Robbie," said Dennis Wu.

"I think you're a shoo-in for the majors one day, Robbie," said Melinda.

"She's right," said Brian. "Robbie's a shoo-in for 'The Show'!"

Patty Sanchez asked, "What's 'The Show'?"

"It's what pro players sometimes call baseball in the major leagues," explained Dennis Wu. "If you think about it, it fits. I mean, what greater show is there than major-league baseball, huh? It's the greatest show on earth!"

"I thought the circus was the greatest show on earth," said Patty.

At this remark, Dennis, Brian, Eagle, Josh, and Robbie just stared at her.

"You're all wrong," said Ralph. "Track is the greatest show on earth, especially when I'm running. Hee-hee."

Everyone at the table laughed. They were still laughing when the waiter came over with the pizza. Rather than order another pie, they decided to recut the one they just got with plastic knives.

"Could we have three more plates, please?" Ralph asked the waiter. "And three more sodas?"

"More plates," grumbled the waiter, heading back to the kitchen. "More sodas."

When he was gone, Cynthia spoke up. "So, Robbie, what do you want to major in at college?"

"Communications," said Robbie, taking a recut slice of pizza. "You know, like journalism, reporting, broadcasting, stuff like that."

"Redstone has a great program in communications!" said Joshua. "There was a big article about it in *American Chronicle* last month."

"What kind of communications department does Lansley have, Rob?" asked Cynthia. She was one of the few people who ever called Robbie "Rob."

"It's a pretty good school. I'm sure it has a fine program in communications," said Robbie.

"You don't know yet?" Cynthia asked, shocked.

"I'll find out. I don't have to decide for a while. A lot depends on how my season goes."

"I'm almost positive I'll be going to Lansley," said Ralph. "Ossie Pickner is there. He's one of the best track coaches in the world! But I say you can't finally tell until you visit a place. I'm going out to Lansley in a month or so and talk to Pickner. They're ready to offer me a full scholarship. I'm sure they'll do the same for Robbie. And I sure wouldn't mind having a friend there!" Ralph clapped Robbie on the back.

"Well, maybe I'll end up going there with you, Ralph!" said Robbie. The idea of going on a long trip away from everything had a strong appeal right now to Robbie.

The waiter came back with three plates and three sodas. When he left, the conversation broke up into smaller groups again.

Robbie was feeling a little uneasy. When he'd been talking about his college plans, he had sensed tension from some of his friends. And he suspected that Cynthia was disappointed in him for not checking out Lansley's communications program.

A table in the middle of Swanee's emptied out. Eagle recognized one of the people now leaving as a friend from his neighborhood. "Excuse me a sec, Cynthia," said Eagle, getting up from his chair and heading for the front door.

"Hey, Eagle!" shouted Brian from the back table. "You're not getting out of the check that easy!" Brian laughed.

Cynthia, however, looked glum. "Typical," she muttered to herself.

"Want to punch up some tunes on the jukebox with me?" Robbie asked her. Cynthia nodded.

Robbie walked up to the jukebox and rolled two quarters into the slot. Then he scanned the selections. Cynthia stood beside him.

"Play M 137," she told him.

"What's M 137?" He was only up to the G selections.

"Old favorite," she said. "Van Morrison's 'Moondance.' "

"Never heard of him—or the song."

"My dad has it on an old 45. Every time he works around the house, he plays it, over and over. After a while, it sunk in. Imagine—liking a song your dad likes. Yeesh!"

"Hey, my dad used to be—" Robbie was about to tell her that Simon Belmont was once a member of the rock band Salty Dogs. But he thought the timing wasn't right. "—into all that old stuff, too."

"Guess it wasn't old to them," said Cynthia. "You know, back then."

"Yeah," said Robbie, pushing M 137 and the buttons for two more songs. "I can't imagine hearing a band like Axle Grease on an oldies station."

Cynthia suddenly grew very serious. "You know, Robbie, you can play baseball *and* learn communications at Redstone."

"Uh, well . . ."

"Well what?" she demanded.

Robbie paused. With Cynthia, he had to say what he meant and mean what he said. "Well, going to a new place and living in a whole different state can teach me something, too. Lansley has a whole different climate. It's warmer, for one thing."

70

"So weather is more important than what you want to study?" Cynthia looked annoyed.

"It just means Lansley's baseball season is a little longer than Redstone's," said Robbie. "Are you mad about something?"

Cynthia's face flushed red. "I just don't like seeing someone I care about being so casual about such an important decision!" she said. Robbie noticed Melinda glancing over at them at this point.

Cynthia went on, her eyes burning into Robbie's. "And maybe there's something else for you at Redstone University—if you were smart enough to notice!"

With that, she walked away in a huff. Robbie looked at Melinda, who was looking at him. He quickly looked away, pretending to search for more tunes on the jukebox.

Robbie couldn't help it—he had a small smile on his face. *She cares!* he thought. *Cynthia still cares about me!* The song "Moondance" was in full swing now. Robbie was surprised at how good it sounded—right this moment.

"What are you smiling at, Robbo?" It was Brian, coming up next to him by the jukebox.

"I think Cynthia is getting tired of Eagle and is interested in me again."

"Not again!" said Brian. "This happens every six months, it seems."

"I guess so, but I have a good feeling about it this time."

"If you're going to Lansley, I wouldn't put

much stock in you and Cynthia," said Brian.

Before Robbie could reply, Brian dropped a bombshell. "I think I realized something tonight, Robbie. I think after ten years or so of knowing her, I'm getting a crush on Melinda! I know, I know, she's going with Josh. But I can't stop thinking about her. All I want to do over there is sit and stare at her!"

Oh, man, thought Robbie. *This whole thing is getting weird! Coach is right—I'm going to need my concentration, on and off the field!*

Chapter Seven

The Riverton Tigers blazed through the first part of their season. Team after team fell to their hot bats and powerful pitching. Their line-up was the envy of the league.

Ty Williams, leadoff batter, got on base over half the time. And the junior shortstop had no errors in the field.

Batting second was Abbie Jacobs, the right fielder. Abbie was a soft-spoken sophomore. He was especially good at the hit-and-run and at avoiding double plays.

Dennis Wu batted third. The classy left fielder nearly always got at least one hit a game.

Robbie batted cleanup. Coach Franklin's drills and workouts were paying off. At the plate, Robbie tracked pitches like a cat ready to pounce on a mouse. He was in a good hitting groove.

On the field, Robbie felt on top of every play. Before each pitch, he was mentally prepared for any situation. He called out clear instructions to his fielders. "One out! Lefty up! Ty, you take the throw if he steals. Get two on the ground ball! Heads up, now!"

Eddie Mosely, the muscle-bound first baseman, batted fifth in Riverton's line-up. He added a powerful long-ball threat to the offense. Opposing pitchers didn't walk Robbie as often as they would have liked because of Eddie.

Third baseman Sam Thorne batted sixth. The freshman's mild manner disappeared when he batted. His swing was ferocious, and his screaming line drives often brought Robbie home.

Todd Murphy, the Tigers' small but alert junior second baseman, batted seventh. His average was a respectable .285. Only Ty and Robbie had more stolen bases than Todd.

The sophomore center fielder, Chris "Cat" Malone, batted eighth. Apart from the pitcher, Cat was the weakest hitter in the starting line-up. But he was a devoted team player and an excellent fielder. He took extra batting practice every chance he got, and his hitting started to improve a little.

Bill Wirick batted ninth. His batting wasn't as good as his pitching. But he had the ability to hit a long ball every once in a while. Wire was also an excellent bunter, something he practiced every day.

Wire's pitching was just short of awesome so far this year. It was easy for Robbie to call pitches for such a strong pitcher.

Riverton's relief pitcher this year was Ned Burney. He had starred on Riverton's basketball team during the winter. The tall sophomore had a late-breaking curve and a sinking fast ball.

Being the Tiger captain was a relief for Robbie. It gave his mind a rest from his off-field problems. The rest of his life felt so confusing that Robbie couldn't wait to get to practice or a game. Baseball meant he could clear his mind and do something he liked and knew how to do.

For example, he didn't know what to do when Brian talked to him about how pretty Melinda looked. But he knew exactly what to do when the cleanup batter for the Reddington Rockets came up with the bases loaded in the ninth inning.

Robbie called for Wire's overhand sinker. The batter had already missed it four times during the game. The batter grounded it to Ty Williams. Ty flipped it to Todd Murphy at second for one out. Todd made his usual graceful pivot and fired to Eddie Mosely for a game-ending double play. Simple!

Not simple was knowing what to say to Dennis Wu when he told Robbie that Cynthia had broken up with Eagle for good. But when Wire walked two straight batters against the Captown Dukes, Robbie knew just what to say. He trotted to the mound and told Wire to stop rushing his delivery. "That way, we can all get home in time to watch the Titans' game on TV," he said. Wire smiled and nodded. He mowed down the next two batters on strikes. Easy as pie!

But the most helpless Robbie felt was before the Tigers' game with the Fulton Bucks. His father's eyesight had gotten a lot better. Simon wanted to try driving. He decided to drive Robbie the short distance to Riverton High School. They went out the driveway, then down the block. As they came to the first stop sign, a delivery truck approached the intersection. Before it crossed, Simon started to drive forward. "Dad! Watch it!" Robbie yelled.

Mr. Belmont slammed on the brakes. Robbie's head grazed the sun visor that he had flipped down at the start of the trip. Mr. Belmont quickly backed the car out of the way. The truck driver gave them an angry look as he passed. But Simon didn't see it. He was looking down. His hand was on his forehead and he was breathing hard.

Simon Belmont turned to his son and said, "Sorry, Robbie. You okay?"

"Yeah, I'm all right."

"Good thing we were wearing seat belts."

"I'll say." Robbie flipped up the sun visor his head had brushed against.

"I just didn't see him. I didn't see that huge truck!" Simon gulped a few times. "I shouldn't be driving," he said softly. "I'm kidding myself. My eyes aren't better. I just *want* them to be better."

"Still blurry?" Robbie asked.

"Not all blurry. Just my side vision, I guess."

They sat quietly. Robbie wondered what he

could do. He put his hand on his father's shoulder. Simon patted it gratefully.

"You'd better drive me home, Robbie."

Things sure can change fast, Robbie thought grimly as he took over the driving. *Early last summer, Dad taught me how to drive. Now, he can hardly see well enough to drive down the block!*

Robbie pulled into their driveway. Simon got out slowly. "I'll get your mom," he said.

Robbie felt very sad as he watched his father walk to the house. In a minute, his mother came out. Robbie said, "I'll drive to school, Mom. You can drive the car back."

Ellen nodded and got in the front seat. As she put her seat belt on, Robbie heard her sniffle. "Are you all right, Mom?" he asked.

"No. But I'll be okay."

Robbie started driving. They came to the stop sign where Simon had almost had the accident. Ellen Belmont said, "He has to see a new doctor today."

"What new doctor?" Robbie asked, driving on.

"A nerve doctor. A neurologist."

"Why? It's an eye disease, isn't it?"

"The eye doctor suggested we see a nerve doctor," she said. "Your father's optic neuritis might be a sign of something else."

"Something worse?"

"No one seems to know yet."

Robbie nodded. He didn't know what to do or say. He parked the car in the school lot. His mother smiled and patted him on the back. He pecked her cheek and got out of the car. She got into the driver's seat. As she drove away, she called, "Get lots of hits!" It was then that Robbie realized both his parents would miss today's game.

Robbie was angry—at what, he wasn't quite certain. But he took out his anger against the Fulton Bucks. The first good pitch he got in the game, he smashed over the left-field fence. The Fulton left fielder watched the ball as if it were a shooting star. It was a tremendous home run.

The next time up, Robbie golfed a very low fast ball high into center field. It, too, cleared the fence by a wide margin. And in the seventh inning, when he batted for the third time, Robbie slugged a frozen-rope triple. Had he managed to get under the ball a little bit more, it would surely have been his third homer of the day. The ball hit a fence post and bounced back thirty yards!

Robbie never got to hit in the ninth inning, though he came to the plate for the fourth and last time. The Bucks' pitcher threw four straight balls *way* outside, so Robbie couldn't so much as lunge his bat at them. The Fulton pitcher seemed quite happy to walk him intentionally.

Defensively, Robbie was just as impressive. Only one Fulton runner tried to steal on him. He was halfway from first to second base when Robbie's furious throw zoomed into Ty's glove. After that, no other Buck tried to steal.

Once the game was over, Robbie showered

78

and hurried home. He found his mother and father eating sandwiches in the kitchen.

"Hi, Robbie," said Simon. "How many hits?"

"Three for four. Two homers, a triple, and a walk," Robbie said. "We won, 6–2."

"Don't you ever hit singles anymore?" his mother asked.

"What'd the new doctor say?" Robbie asked.

"She said optic neuritis could be a sign of many things," answered Simon. "Some of them bad, some of them not so bad. She wanted to know every single health problem I've ever had. Then she tested my speech, my eyes, my face, my tongue, my throat, my hearing, my sense of touch, my coordination, my reflexes, and finally my posture! She tested everything but my eyelashes!"

"They won't have the results of the tests for a while," added Ellen Belmont. "They also might want to do more tests before making a diagnosis."

"What do they think it might be?" asked Robbie.

"They suspect a couple of things, but they're not sure yet," said his father.

"What 'couple of things'?" Robbie asked.

"We'll know in a week or two," said his mother.

"Meanwhile," his father said, "I think the best thing for us to do is go on living!"

Robbie smiled, but he was worried. *Why won't they tell me what the "couple of things" are?* he wondered.

Later that night, he made his usual juice run

to the kitchen. As he passed his parents' room, he heard a loud voice. His father was talking.

"Doctors, hospitals, medicine, private nurses, tests, they all cost money! We could be looking at bills adding up to a hundred thousand dollars— maybe more—over the next couple of years! And my university insurance will only pay part of it!"

"Shh, calm down, honey," came his mother's voice. "We don't know for sure yet that's what you have."

The sound of his mother's voice got Robbie moving again. He went into the kitchen feeling horrible. *What disease are they talking about?* he wondered. It was bad enough having some mysterious disease. But they also seemed afraid of losing a lot of money.

Would that mean Robbie couldn't go to college? He had been offered full athletic scholarships to Lansley and Redstone. Tuition was no problem. But there were many other college costs. A full athletic scholarship wouldn't cover everything.

Maybe I should think about making money instead of going to college, Robbie suddenly thought. The idea made him put down his juice for a few seconds.

Coach Franklin had said some scouts were interested in signing Robbie up for pro ball after high school. But Coach Franklin had not been enthusiastic. He definitely wanted Robbie to go to college.

So did Robbie's parents. And so did Robbie! What should he do?

Slipping back to bed, Robbie decided to ask Coach Franklin to invite the scouts to the Tigers' next game.

Chapter Eight

Riverton's next game was against the Park Hill Panthers. They were the Tigers' strongest competition for the league championship this year. The Panthers were a hustling, good-hitting team. They had a promising sophomore pitcher, a lefty named Drew Burke. His teammates called him Onion. Robbie asked Park Hill's catcher why they called their pitcher Onion. "Because his fast ball will make you cry!" came the short reply.

Burke had one of the liveliest fast balls Robbie had ever seen. It was speedy enough to give a batter only half a breath to decide whether to swing or not. And to make matters worse, the fast ball had a different hop to it each time.

Dennis Wu fouled off four of these hopping fast balls before finally swinging at air for strike three. Dennis passed Robbie as Robbie went to the plate. "It either jumps, sails, dips, or veers," mumbled Dennis. "You never know which."

Burke's first pitch to Robbie veered outside for ball one. The second sailed to the high outside strike zone. Robbie stepped right into it and swung. It hit the meat of the bat and sailed out of the park. But it curved foul by two feet at the last moment.

Riverton fans jumped to their feet, then groaned. Robbie smiled. *We'll see who's crying at the end of the game, Onion!*

The next pitch was another hopping fast ball. This time, it dipped at the last moment to the low inside corner. *Ahh!* Robbie thought. He swung with such smooth power that the crowd also went "Ahh!" Their "Ahh!" grew into a roar as Robbie's hit ripped down the left-field line. It hit the fence on two bounces. Robbie slid into second base with a double.

As he dusted off his pants, he enjoyed the crowd's applause. For a few minutes there, he hadn't worried about his father once!

From second base, he could see a group of scouts in the front rows behind the plate. It was easy to tell they were scouts because a few of them had radar guns to time the speed of pitches. And all the scouts had stopwatches and notebooks. Robbie was sure every scout had timed his sprint to first base. He also knew his speed would have impressed them. Melinda had already timed him. He made it to first in 3.6 seconds. That was faster than most major-league players!

Robbie knew speed was the first thing scouts

looked for. Most baseball talents were useful either for offense or in the field. But speed was useful for both offense and defense. Robbie had solid, strong legs, the kind scouts looked for in a catcher. But he also had the long stride and grace of a major-league outfielder. It was a rare combination. Robbie's batting power and smart, strong catching interested the scouts a lot.

Robbie knew the scouts also liked Bill Wirick. The scouts' radar guns were timing Wire's fast ball at eighty-four miles per hour. This was not major-league speed, but one day it could be.

The scouts were also watching Ty Williams, even though he was only a junior. Ty held the school record for most games played without an error: fifty-six so far. This was all the more impressive because he played shortstop. A shortstop has far more fielding chances than any other position.

Ty's smooth fielding amazed Robbie. Talk about concentration! Ty's steady gaze seemed to lock on every ball hit to him. His whole body glided calmly to the right place with no wasted movements. The ball seemed to hop into his glove like a rabbit into a hole.

At the plate, Ty had a great ability to get on base and score. He had cracked a sharp single to center field to start the inning. He then moved to third base on Robbie's double. Ty was definitely someone the scouts were keeping an eye on.

But Robbie was the main reason the scouts were there. It wasn't just because of his talents, which were many. There was another reason. The major leagues needed catchers.

Catchers have always been in short supply for professional baseball. But over the past five years, the major leagues had developed an even greater need for catchers than ever. Coach Franklin had told Robbie that scouts now had a very strong call out to find catchers.

One scout who wanted to offer Robbie a bonus for signing right out of high school was in the stands today. His name was Tilly Goodman. Robbie easily identified Tilly by the brown and gold Los Angeles Lions' baseball cap he wore. Tilly had been told that the Lions needed catchers and they needed them now! As Robbie stood on second, he could see Tilly look at him. He could see a smile on Tilly's face, even from that distance.

Muscular Eddie Mosely took a home-run swing at Burke's fast ball. He missed it badly.

"We call that one the Onion Dip," said the Panther catcher, snickering. "Get it?"

Eddie said nothing. The next pitch was another dipping fast ball. Eddie swung and ripped it between the shortstop and third baseman for a ground-ball single. From first base, Eddie called to the catcher, "Mosely hit. Get it?"

As for Robbie, he was off at the crack of the bat. The ball bounced a yard in front of him as he tore to third. Ty scored easily. It would be close if Robbie tried to score.

As Robbie ran to third, he could see Coach

Franklin squinting into left field, trying to decide if Robbie could make it. When Robbie was a yard from the bag, the coach started waving his arms like a windmill. "Go, Robbie! You got it!" he yelled.

Robbie stepped on the inside corner of the third-base bag and sped for home. His long, strong legs chewed up the distance. Sam Thorne, the Tigers' next batter, stood close behind the catcher and umpire. Robbie looked at Sam for help. Sam threw his arms to the right and yelled, "Slide!" Robbie did a hook slide in the direction Sam pointed. His body passed the catcher. Then Robbie uncurled his leg. His foot brushed over the plate as he passed.

He was clearly safe. *But does the ump agree?* he wondered. "Safe!" called the umpire.

"Way to go, Speedo!" yelled Sam Thorne, giving Robbie a high five.

Robbie jogged happily to the bench. He noticed Tilly Goodman in his L.A. Lions' cap standing and clapping with the rest of the crowd.

Wire pitched steady and strong. The Panthers got a run in the fourth after Wire gave up his first walk. Drew Burke helped his own cause with a double. Only a great throw by Riverton center fielder Cat Malone kept it from being a triple.

The scouts saw Robbie's best catching play in the top of the seventh inning. The Tigers were ahead, 2–1. There was one out, and the Panthers had men on first and third.

Robbie watched carefully as the batter took the signal from the third-base coach. The batter stared a little longer than usual at the coach for the sign. Then Robbie saw the same Panther coach whisper something to the runner on third. The runner on third took a deep breath and nodded.

Something's up, Robbie thought. *And I think it's a suicide squeeze*. He called for a pitchout.

Sure enough, as Wire delivered, both runners took off as the batter squared around to bunt. Wire threw a beautiful pitchout, fast and too high outside for the hitter to get his bat on.

The runner coming in from third stopped as soon as he saw it was a pitchout. Robbie stepped to his right and caught the ball. He started to throw it to Sam Thorne at third. Sam had not run in for the bunt because Wire had signaled to him that a pitchout was coming.

The runner stopped. If Robbie threw the ball, the runner would try for home.

Robbie sprinted at the runner. Wire ran in to cover the plate. Robbie kept going until the runner had to turn and run for third or be tagged. *Then* Robbie tossed it to Sam. The runner stopped and ran toward Robbie again. Sam snapped the ball to Robbie. The runner ran right into Robbie's tag.

Without hesitating, Robbie fired the ball to Todd Murphy covering second base. The other runner had stolen second but had wandered a few steps off the bag. Robbie's fast toss caught him by surprise. Double play!

"Now *that's* heads-up ball, Robbie!" shouted Coach Franklin. The coach had called out three compliments to Robbie this game. That was two more than he had in any other game this year!

In the final innings, Abbie Jacobs, Wire, and Robbie hit solo home runs. The Tigers won the game, 5–1.

It had been a red-hot day for Robbie. All the scouts wanted to talk with him after the game. But Coach Franklin only allowed three of them to meet with him.

The meetings were held in the office of Riverton's principal. Coach Franklin and the principal were there. They would make sure all the recruiting rules were obeyed.

The first scout was Mack Doogan. Coach Franklin introduced him as an old friend. Mack had a craggy, kind face. He praised Robbie for the great game he played. He said the Titans were interested in him whenever he decided to turn pro. Mack also spoke highly of Redstone University.

"It's worth at least a couple of years in the minors," Mack said. "Frank Preston is the best coach you can hope for—besides Gus here, of course." The two old friends gave each other wry smiles.

Robbie liked Mack. There didn't seem to be anything phony or pushy about him.

The next scout's name was Norman Taylor. He had ties through Lansley University with three major-league teams. Norman talked about all the players he had brought to Lansley who had gone on to professional baseball.

Robbie asked him about Lansley's communications program. "They have a big new communications building," Norman said.

The principal spoke up. "I wasn't aware of that."

"Oh, yeah," said Norman Taylor. "It's brand new. Big article on it in a national magazine. Can't think of the name offhand."

The third scout was Tilly Goodman. He just had a short piece to say, but it had a strong effect.

"Great game, kid. Great swinging. I heard you almost got called out on strikes your first game this year. Should've been, I heard, but the ump gave you a welcome-back gift. When I heard that, you know, I almost didn't come to see you. But the coach tells me you had a year layoff, it was your first time up, blah blah.

"Well, I'm glad I did come. You swing like a champ in there, kid! Great backstopping, too. I'll tell you something. You've got what we scouts call 'the face.' It's just a look you have, a major-league look. It's hard to describe. But you got it. And the Lions are looking for catchers, Robbie. Hoo-ee, are they ever!"

Tilly took off his Lions' cap and fanned himself with it. "And as you probably know, we also have first pick in the draft this June. Now I understand from Gus Franklin here that you plan to go to college. All I want to say is, the Lions will be glad to pay and arrange for you to get a college degree *while playing pro ball with us*! If you would sign with us right out of high school, do you know how much bonus money you might want?"

"Now wait a minute, Tilly," Coach Franklin said, leaning forward in his chair.

"I'm allowed to ask him that, Gus. Here's the official form. See that—it says 'signability.' I'm allowed to ask him what bonus he might expect upon signing."

The principal said, "You *can* ask, Mr. Goodman, but you *cannot* say whether you'd be willing to pay the amount he names. No contract discussion can begin until the June draft. You know that."

"I won't respond, sir, I assure you," said Tilly, putting his cap over his heart. "I've been a scout since the baseball draft began. I know the rules."

"And the ropes!" said Coach Franklin. He still wasn't satisfied. "Look, Tilly, say Robbie would name a figure. He'd be able to tell by your reaction whether you're willing to pay it or not."

"What do you want me to do, Gus?" Tilly asked. "Do you want me to hide behind that door while Robbie here calls out his signability figure?"

"Robbie will talk it over with all the people he needs to talk it over with," said the coach. "Then, if he does want to consider your offer and if he does come up with a bonus figure, he'll tell me. Then my secretary will relay it to your answering machine. Period!"

"One hundred thousand dollars," said Robbie.

The three adults turned around and gaped at Robbie with their mouths open.

"Robbie!" snapped the coach, after a pause.

"One hundred thousand dollars, Mr. Goodman," said Robbie. "That's my signability figure."

"Hmm, one hundred thousand dollars," said Tilly. Smiling broadly, he wrote the number down on the form. Robbie felt sure Tilly thought such a bonus quite possible.

"Darn it, Tilly, at least stop grinning," said Gus Franklin. "Listen, that figure is not firm. For one thing, he has to discuss it with his parents first."

"If it changes," said Tilly, putting his cap back on, "give me a call. I would love to meet your parents, Robbie. Here's my card. I'll be in touch. Thank you all." He touched a finger to the bill of his cap and left the room.

"Just what do you think you're doing, Robbie?" asked Coach Franklin testily.

"I'd like to know, too," said the principal, only slightly less annoyed.

"My dad has an eye problem," said Robbie slowly. "No one knows exactly what it is yet. At least, no one has told *me* exactly what it is yet. Anyway, I overheard my dad say it might cost a hundred thousand dollars or more for treatment over the next couple of years." Here, Robbie looked directly at Gus Franklin. "Coach, we don't have that kind of money."

"What about medical insurance?" asked the principal.

"It'll pay part," said Robbie.

"I see," said the principal.

"You know, Robbie, you could have told us this *before* we met with these scouts today," said Coach Franklin. He walked over to the window and peered out. Then he turned around to face Robbie. "You still should talk it over with your parents."

"I know," said Robbie. "I will."

"A hundred thousand dollars," said the principal, giving a low whistle. "My, my."

Chapter Nine

"So what happened when you talked it over with your parents?" Cynthia Wu asked Robbie.

It was a warm, spring night. They were strolling through the Riverton amusement park, eating cotton candy. It was their first date in over a year. Dennis Wu had told Robbie that Cynthia would be home from Redstone University on spring break. Robbie couldn't stop thinking about asking her out, so he finally did! She had agreed cheerfully.

"I've never seen my parents' faces go through so many changes in such a short time," said Robbie. "First, they laughed. They thought I was making a little joke. Then they realized I wasn't kidding and they looked shocked. My dad got a little angry. He said, 'A college education is worth more than money, son. I want you to go to a college with a campus! Not college by mail and off-season tutorials! I don't care if they offer a billion dollars.'"

"Did your mother agree with that?" Cynthia asked.

"She did. She nodded. She put her hand on Dad's back. She wanted him to calm down."

The two came to an empty bench. "Let's sit for a while, Robbie. I want to know more about this."

"Look!" said Robbie, as Cynthia sat down. "There's the baseball toss! Let me knock some bottles over for you first."

Without waiting for Cynthia, Robbie rushed ahead. By the time Cynthia got to the booth, Robbie was already chucking balls at the stacked metal bottles.

The middle-aged man running the booth wore a Riverton Tigers' baseball cap. He obviously knew Robbie. He grinned broadly when Robbie knocked over five stacks with five throws. As he handed Robbie his prize, a stuffed penguin, the man said, "Knock 'em dead in tomorrow's game, Robbie." Robbie thanked him politely.

Robbie proudly handed the penguin to Cynthia. His face fell when Cynthia said, "No thanks. You keep it." She turned and walked away from him.

"Me?" Robbie said to her back. He was baffled by her reaction. "I don't keep stuffed animals!"

"Neither do I," she said, turning and walking toward him.

"I thought you'd appreciate it," said Robbie. "I won it for you."

"For me? You didn't even ask me. You walked away in the middle of an important conversation."

"I don't want this stupid thing!" Robbie said loudly. He waved the penguin over his head by its cloth beak.

"Don't, mister!" a small voice piped up behind him. "You'll hurt him!"

Robbie turned and saw a little girl looking sadly at the penguin he was shaking. "Oh, I'm sorry," Robbie said to her, his anger disappearing. "Mr. Pengy and I like to play like that."

"His name is not Mr. Pengy," said the girl softly. "It's Petey."

"Petey?" said Cynthia with a surprised laugh.

The little girl was standing beside her older brother. He was looking around, not interested in what his little sister was doing.

Robbie held the toy up to his ear. "What's that you say, Pengy, I mean, Petey? Uh-huh. Okay, if that's what you want." Robbie now looked at the little girl. "Petey here says that he's looking for a new home. But he won't go with anyone unless it's a little girl named . . . named . . . " Robbie again put the penguin's mouth close to his ear.

"My name's Belinda!" said the little girl hopefully.

"No!" blurted Robbie, blinking in surprise. "I can't believe it! Ol' Petey just whispered to me that he won't go home with anyone but a little girl named Belinda." He handed the stuffed penguin over to her. "Promise you'll take good care of him?"

"Oh, I will, I will," said Belinda gleefully,

clutching the toy in her arms. "Thank you, mister."

Her brother yanked her arm. "Come on, Belinda!" he urged. "The baseball booth's open!" They both ran to the booth Robbie had just left.

"I'm still a little ticked at you," Cynthia said, "even if you did find Petey a good home."

"Sometimes I feel I can't do anything right with you."

"Robbie, you have to concentrate with me at least as much as you do on the field!"

This made Robbie pause. It made sense. "Okay. I'm sorry. Let's sit, then," he said.

They went back to the bench Cynthia had sat on earlier.

"My hands are sticky from the cotton candy," Robbie said.

"Mine, too," said Cynthia. She held up her hand and looked at it. Robbie pressed his palm and fingers against hers. They pulled them slowly apart. The stickiness glued their skin a little.

Then Robbie said, "Anyway, I suggested that my bonus money could help pay for dad's medical expenses. My parents looked surprised. I told them I had accidentally heard them talking about not being able to afford Dad's treatment. Mom said it was nice to know we might have that much money if we needed it. But that seemed to make my dad really mad. He stormed out of the room."

"I can understand him being mad," Cynthia said.

"I can't!" said Robbie. "You'd think he'd be grateful."

"Robbie, the last thing he wants is for you to miss out on a regular college education. Remember, he's a college professor himself. You know how much it means to him!"

Robbie was quiet for a moment. "Sometimes you're a little spooky, Cynthia," he said. "That's almost the same thing my mother said."

Cynthia said nothing for a while. Then she asked, "Did your father stay mad?"

"No. A half hour later, he apologized for getting so angry. He told me he was real proud of my baseball success and all. He said my offer was real generous, but they'd find a way to pay for the expenses. He said I shouldn't worry about it.

"I said it would be my money and I'd do what I wanted with it. Then he started fuming again. He didn't yell or anything. He just said good night and walked away. My mother said they didn't even know if they would need money or not. My dad still has to take more tests."

"Rob, if your folks say they can manage the money, maybe you should believe them. Let them take care of that, and you do what you think best."

"Go to Lansley?"

"If that's what you think is best," said Cynthia. She didn't look happy with the idea. "Have you found out yet what kind of communications program Lansley has?"

"Their recruiter said they had a great program."

"Did you read the Lansley catalogue?"

"Uh, well, no."

"What?" Cynthia asked. "You still haven't looked it up? I can't believe you sometimes, Robbie!"

"Could we maybe finish this conversation on the ferris wheel?" he asked.

"Maybe we should," she answered.

They walked to the ferris wheel and Robbie bought tickets. They climbed in. The attendant locked the restraining bar in front of them.

As usual on the ferris wheel, Robbie was surprised how scary it actually was. It always looked so peaceful and pretty when seen from a distance. But the creaking and rocking so high up made Robbie catch his breath a few times. He tried not to let Cynthia notice. But Cynthia didn't miss much.

"It's a little frightening, isn't it?" she said. "Although in an *enjoyable* way." She slipped her arm through Robbie's and moved closer. *All right!* thought Robbie. They rocked and circled a few minutes without talking, enjoying the sensation and sights.

Cynthia had just put her head on Robbie's shoulder when the ferris wheel suddenly stopped. They were at the top. Their car rocked violently.

"This is the scariest part," said Cynthia, cuddling closer.

"The scariest part is worrying about Dad losing his sight," said Robbie.

"We'll have to see what the doctors say, I guess," said Cynthia.

"Meanwhile, I have to make a decision," said Robbie.

"You don't have to decide until June. You have a lot of different things to consider. At least wait until the doctors make a diagnosis."

"Hmm. And maybe I should think more about Redstone. Dad might need me closer to home."

"I'll be glad to help, too, you know. In any way I can."

"Thanks, Cynthia."

The ferris wheel moved down a notch and stopped again. As the carriages rocked, Robbie could hear other passengers whooping in mock fear. Robbie said, "But if I do go to college, I could lose my chance for that bonus money. I could get injured, or I could even lose my baseball talent. It happens, you know. A lot of high-school baseball stars turn out to be duds in college. Then I'd end up with no bonus or anything. What if my dad needs money then?"

"You don't have to worry about losing your baseball talent, Robbie," Cynthia said.

"Well, that's nice of you to say, but—"

"But nothing, Robbie," said Cynthia firmly. "I'm not just flattering you. I knew it the first day I saw you and Eddie Trent talking together in your freshman year. It was after the county championship game, when you had that incredible day. I saw that you and Eddie both had the same kind of look. It's hard to describe. But what it means is you're both born baseball players. I thought everybody could see it."

Robbie realized Cynthia was talking about what Tilly Goodman had called "the face."

The ferris wheel lurched down another place. They sat there rocking. "Still, if I think my folks need that money, I'm going to sign with the Lions," Robbie said. "I don't care what my parents think—as long as Dad gets better! It's my life, and I'll live it the way I want to!" said Robbie.

The carriage they were in finally moved to ground level. The attendant unlocked the restraining bar. Robbie and Cynthia got out, neither speaking with the other. They both walked fast, about a yard apart. They said nothing until they walked out the amusement park gate. Then Cynthia stopped. Her dark eyes flashed.

"Yes, it is your life, Robbie, but your life involves other people! You can't just cut us out of the picture. No one's trying to make you do anything stupid! We just want you to consider everything in a reasonable way."

"I am," said Robbie defensively.

"No, you're not!" said Cynthia. "You have other talents besides baseball, Robbie."

"Yeah? Like what?"

"Like writing. I read those articles you wrote for the high-school paper last year. They were really good. And your writing will only get better at college."

Last baseball season, when Robbie was still recovering from his thumb injury, he covered a few Tiger games for the school paper. The sports editor, Jerry Swift, was a friend of Robbie's and had been very helpful. Robbie had received a number of compliments about his articles. Even Coach Franklin said it was the best reporting of Tiger baseball he had ever read.

Robbie was secretly pleased to hear how much Cynthia had liked his writing. But he felt stubborn right now. "You don't understand," he said.

"I *do* understand. And you know I do! I understand you might be offered a sum of money that would gag a horse, a sum of money most people our age can't even imagine. I know you've been dreaming of playing major-league baseball since you were a kid. And I know you feel you have to help your father, and this seems like the only way to do that. But I also know you have to respect your parents' wishes.

"Remember how angry you were last year when I asked Eagle to my senior prom? It looked like you and I were finished then. But *I* never thought so. Not really. And it wasn't because of baseball either. It was because of those articles you wrote. I was . . . impressed. I admit it. And you have to keep working on that ability, Robbie. You have to go to college any way you can. You can be *really* great—not just in baseball, but in your whole life!"

Everything Cynthia said made perfect sense to Robbie. But for some reason, he didn't want to admit it. It made him feel too emotional.

"You don't understand," he said again.

"Okay. I tried to be honest with you, and you don't want that. So now, I'll just say something stupid. I'll say good-bye."

She turned and stalked off.

Robbie just stood there, watching. He felt miserable. His world seemed to be falling apart everywhere except on the baseball field.

Chapter Ten

The Riverton Tigers were having a glorious season, and Robbie Belmont was at the center of it. The team continued to cut down league opponents like a power mower rolling through grass. Robbie's batting average soared above the .500 mark. The league pitchers seemed like batting practice pitchers to him. Catching, he had no errors, no passed balls, and no steals on him since the first game! He thought of himself as a pro among amateurs. He was playing so well that he began to think even college competition would be too easy for him.

Despite his success on the field, Robbie was far from happy. Try as he might, he couldn't stop thinking of Cynthia Wu. He missed her a lot. He often made up conversations with her in his head. He tried phoning her a few times after their fight at the amusement park. But she was either "out" or "too busy" to answer his calls. He stopped making them. Then Dennis Wu told him Cynthia was going with Eagle Wilson again!

Another thing that made Robbie unhappy was his father's hardships. Simon Belmont's eye problem was not getting worse, but it wasn't getting better either. He still couldn't read, drive a car, or watch TV. He hadn't attended any of Robbie's baseball games this season and seemed to be tired all the time. The neurologist still hadn't made a final diagnosis yet. She wanted Simon to take two more series of tests first, including a spinal tap. It was hard on the whole family not knowing what Simon had.

Robbie could usually talk things over with one of his friends, and that would help a lot. But none of his friends seemed available.

Ralph was on a trip visiting Lansley University. Robbie had wanted to go with Ralph. But he didn't want to leave his parents alone. Also, the Riverton baseball season got in the way.

Josh Kenny was away at Redstone University. Robbie knew he could have called him up, but he didn't. It didn't seem natural to Robbie.

Besides, part of the problem for Robbie was Josh's girlfriend, Melinda. It used to be that Robbie and Melinda could talk and be together for hours at a time. But there was something about the way Melinda looked at Robbie now that made him uncomfortable after just a short while. He'd think of the flimsiest excuse to leave earlier than usual—that's how bad it had become.

Brian Webster and Robbie had been best friends since fifth grade. They had always confided in one another, told each other things they'd never tell anyone else. But since Brian confessed his secret crush on Melinda, Robbie couldn't discuss the "Melinda problem" with him at all.

Robbie also didn't feel it would be right to talk about his feelings for Cynthia with her younger brother, Dennis. So that left him out. And though he was friendly with Jerry Swift through their work on the school paper last year, Robbie felt he didn't know Jerry well enough yet.

More and more, Robbie felt his life was getting away from him. What got him through so far was baseball. It kept his spirits up. There were days when he'd be at practice two hours ahead of the other players. And usually he stayed for an extra hour's worth of batting practice.

As much as Robbie looked forward to practice now, he *lived* for the weekend games. The click of pressure in the bat when he homered stopped him from worrying about life after graduation. The puff of dust a Wire fast ball made in his mitt kept him from thinking about Melinda's odd behavior. Baseball seemed to offer something to save him from distraction and worry.

Another example of how baseball kept him from going crazy came in the Tigers' second game with the Fulton Bucks. Robbie was sitting on the bench, unbuckling his shin guards. Brian was talking to him.

"I'm going to tell her, Robbie. I'm going to tell Melinda tonight how much I like her. What's the worst that can happen? All right, all right, plenty!

She could laugh in my face, and we'd avoid each other for the rest of our lives. Is it worth the risk?"

Robbie unsnapped the last buckle. He was due on deck. "I don't think she'd laugh at you, Bri." Robbie grabbed his bat and headed up the dugout steps. On the top step, he turned around and said in a low voice, "What about Josh? How's he fit into all this?"

"I thought he and Melinda had this sort of understanding between them," said Brian uncertainly. "You know, that they could date others if they wanted to."

"Yeah, I heard that, too." Robbie peered over his shoulder at home plate. Dennis Wu had just swung and missed for strike two. "Look, I've got to get going. I'm no expert in these matters, believe me. It's your call—all the way. Know what I mean?"

"Yeah, I know," said Brian, nodding toward the on-deck circle. "Better take a few cuts before heading in. The way you've been hitting, you'll need them!"

Robbie grinned. He knew Brian was joking. Robbie had nine hits in his last ten at-bats!

Robbie stepped into the on-deck circle and slipped a lead ring around the end of his bat. He took a couple of swings to loosen up. It was peaceful in the circle. He breathed a sigh of relief.

On a beautiful day for a ball game, the Tigers were ahead, 4–2, in the bottom of the fifth. Robbie looked around the stands. The home crowd was full of bright colors and high spirits.

Then, Robbie spotted his mother sitting by herself in the stands. He quickly looked away and started swinging the bat hard. With each rippling swing, he saw different pictures of his father in his head. First swing, he saw him napping on their couch. Second swing, he saw him on the front porch, savoring the morning air. Third swing, he saw his father last Christmas Eve, happily handing Robbie the very bat he was now swinging! The familiar motion of swinging the bat had turned sadness about his father into thankfulness.

Dennis Wu suddenly cracked a single up the middle. Robbie was now ready. He felt a familiar excitement in the pit of his stomach. It was an excitement that made him feel solid, not nervous.

Robbie took the first pitch for a called strike. He stepped out of the box and looked at the umpire. "Good call," he said. The umpire nodded. In the brief look back, Robbie had noticed a gold and brown cap worn by a spectator. *Tilly Goodman is here again!* thought Robbie. The Los Angeles Lions' scout had been coming to almost every game lately.

Robbie took a deep breath and stepped back up to the plate. The Fulton pitcher was big, but not as big as their pitcher last year, Charles "Chainsaw" McKenzer. It was Chainsaw who had ended Riverton's season with a shutout last year. He had since graduated and was now pitching for a nationally ranked college team in Florida.

The Bucks' pitcher on the mound now was Boone Hacker. He stood six feet three inches tall and weighed around 180 pounds. He didn't growl as Chainsaw used to do. But if looks could kill, Boone Hacker would be number one on the FBI's Most Wanted List.

Robbie didn't look at the pitcher out of one eye as most batters did. He turned both eyes on Hacker and met his fierce gaze straight on. The Fulton pitcher wasn't even looking at his catcher for the sign. He was just standing there on the mound, trying to frighten Robbie.

None of this fazed Robbie. Psych jobs that might have affected him during freshman year didn't affect him now. Hacker gave up the staring contest and went into a half wind-up. He checked Dennis Wu's lead off first, then pitched.

The ball came right at Robbie's head!

Robbie hit the dirt. The pitch whooshed through the space where his head had just been. Robbie picked himself up, brushing the dirt off his uniform. The beanball had left him burning with anger. The plate umpire called to the mound, "One more like that, Hacker, and you're out of the game!"

Robbie used his anger. He took his stance again, steady as ever, only now his body was poised to cut loose.

Hacker didn't say anything. He tried locking eyes with Robbie again, but had to look away.

Robbie's stare was harder than his own. Hacker threw to his first baseman three times, not even coming close to picking Dennis Wu off. Hacker was stalling. He didn't want to pitch to Robbie. But finally he had to.

The next pitch was a low outside curve. Robbie wouldn't have cared if it were a foot over his head. He was pumped. He swung his father's Christmas gift. Every ounce of power he had went into the swing. Every worry and fear, all his frustration and anger exploded into that furious but fully controlled swing.

The ball hit wood in a way Robbie never quite felt before. This swing was special, and Robbie knew it. The ball climbed higher and higher. It was still on a rise as it cleared the center-field fence. It flew over the green field behind the center-field fence. Then it bounced hard and high off the macadam street beyond. A group of girls playing hopscotch were startled by the ball skipping through their chalk-lined game. Finally, the ball slowed on a nearby lawn, coming to a halt by a sprinkler.

Robbie trotted around the bases at a leisurely lope. For the time being, his anger and worries went with that hit ball. Baseball was keeping him sane.

The next edition of the school newspaper had a large headline on the back page: BELMONT BELTS ONE NEARLY 500 FEET!

The Riverton Tigers won their division and

then the league championship without a defeat. Jerry Swift asked Robbie to write an article for the school paper. Robbie said okay. He decided the best way to celebrate the Tigers' championship was to write about the most exciting play of their season. He knew exactly what play that was, too.

Robbie called up Melinda. "Do you have the video of our game with the Blue Pine Grizzlies?" he asked.

"Sure do," she said. "Come on over and we'll give it a look."

It took Robbie only a minute to get to Melinda's. She lived a couple of houses down the street. They went into the TV room. Melinda put the videocassette into the VCR. She was wearing bleached jeans with rips in the knees, and a light blue T-shirt.

"How's your dad these days?" she asked.

"Not good," said Robbie. "His vision is no better even though he's taking those steroids."

"That's the same stuff athletes aren't supposed to take, right?"

"Right. It helps them put on muscle, but it has bad side effects over a long period," said Robbie.

"Has the doctor made a diagnosis yet?"

"Not a firm one. The scary thing is, she says it could be multiple sclerosis. But she can't be sure until she takes even more tests."

"Multiple sclerosis? Isn't that some sort of disease that hits the central nervous system?"

"Yeah. In some cases, it can lead to permanent blindness and to life in a wheelchair." Robbie held his breath for a second, trying to hold back any tears. The idea of his father unable to see and confined to a wheelchair was more than he could bear. "Uh, but that's a small percentage, the doctor told us. Most people with MS get a milder form of it. And he may not even *have* MS. At least, the doctor still isn't sure."

Melinda reached over and took Robbie's hand. The color of her eyes matched her T-shirt. Then, slowly, ever so slowly, she leaned over and kissed him on the lips.

"It'll be all right," Melinda whispered, pulling back from the kiss. "I just know it."

Robbie said nothing. He couldn't speak even if he wanted to. He was in shock. *Did she just do what I think she did*?

Melinda was leaning over for what looked like another kiss when the videocassette sputtered on. The sound of bat meeting ball made them both turn toward the TV. On the screen, Robbie was running around the bases after hitting a homer against the Grizzlies.

"What play did you want to see, Robbie?" Melinda asked, sitting up straight now. She picked a carrot stick out of a bowl on the coffee table and started munching.

"Play?" asked Robbie in a fog. Then he remembered why he was there. "Right. Why, *the* play, of course! Bottom of the fourth inning, no outs, Blue Pine at bat, score tied, 2–2."

Melinda grabbed the remote control and fast-forwarded the tape. They munched carrots as the tape whirred. Robbie was trying to forget about the kiss. He was not having much success. Finally, the tape wound around to the bottom of the fourth.

"Here?" asked Melinda in a soft voice.

"Yes," said Robbie. "Do you remember yet?"

"Wait a minute!" she said suddenly. "I know what this is! This is *the* play! I remember now! Of course!"

On the screen, the Blue Pine batter blooped a short pop fly to left. Dennis Wu ran in from left field to catch it. Ty Williams ran out from short-stop. The runners on first and second held their positions, waiting to see if the ball would be caught.

Later that night, eating cookies and sipping milk at his own kitchen table, Robbie wrote a description of the play. It began with third base-man Sam Thorne calling for Ty Williams to catch the blooper fly. The ball bounced out of the Riverton shortstop's diving glove, but left fielder Dennis Wu managed to catch it before it hit the ground. That was one out.

Dennis tried to pick the runner off at second base. But the ball hit the runner's foot and went into center field. At this point, both runners took off, thinking the ball wouldn't be caught and thrown in time to nab them. Cat Malone, how-ever, lived up to his name. He rushed in, bare-handed the scooting ball, and fired it to Sam

Thorne. Sam tagged the runner sliding into third for the second out.

When the runner heading from first to second saw Todd Murphy straddling second base to take Sam Thorne's throw, he hesitated. Then the runner beat a hasty retreat back to first base. Todd took Sam's toss and whipped the ball to Eddie Mosely at first.

But the ball sailed over Eddie's head. It would have been a sure error had not right fielder Abbie Jacobs positioned himself behind Eddie. Abbie speared the ball and flicked it quickly to Eddie, who put the tag on the sliding runner for the third out. Except for the pitcher and catcher, every Tiger fielder had a hand in this triple play.

Robbie was exhausted after finishing the article. He left his notes and notebook right there on the kitchen table and went to bed.

Robbie got up early the next morning. He still felt tired but couldn't sleep. It was just past dawn. Through his open bedroom window, Robbie could smell the fresh air of a late spring day.

Robbie almost always woke up slowly. He was barely able to think or talk until he had some breakfast in him. Something looked different, but he wasn't sure yet. The kitchen light was on, and there was coffee already perking in the pot. That all seemed normal, although it was rather early. Simon Belmont was up. That was normal, too.

"Hi, Dad," mumbled Robbie, pulling the refrigerator door open. He took the pitcher of juice out, shut the door, and got a glass. The feeling that there was something a little unusual still stayed with him.

"Hi, Robbie," his dad said back.

Robbie drank his glass of juice and leaned against the kitchen sink, smacking his lips. Then he saw his dad holding the pages Robbie wrote last night.

"Sorry for leaving the mess on the table, Dad," he said. His voice was starting to sound clearer now. "Want me to put it away?"

"No, no," said Simon, his eyes sparkling. "You know, this is quite good. You write better than some of the English majors I had in class."

Robbie's father seemed happy. "Your mother and I assumed you inherited her athletic ability. But now it looks like you might have inherited something from your old man, too!"

Suddenly, Robbie realized what was unusual. He nearly dropped his juice glass.

"Dad!"

"What?" Simon was still smiling.

"You . . . you read it! You sat there and read it! You're reading again! Is that right? Or am I still half-asleep?"

St. Simon Belmont's smile grew broader. "You may still be half-asleep, Robbie, but I *can* see today. Actually, I started seeing a little better yesterday. I didn't say anything because I didn't want to get everyone's hopes up. But today I woke up, opened the door, smelled the air, and saw a barn swallow on the phone wire across the street. I picked up the morning paper—and I could read the headlines! I came in here and read your article! Not a bad day so far, huh?"

Robbie walked over to his father and gave him a bear hug. Then the two of them woke up Robbie's mother and told her the news. The Belmonts had their own triple play of happiness that morning.

Chapter Eleven

Simon's vision had cleared up. That night, he was able to finish reading a novel he had put down months ago. Over the course of the next week, his vision remained clear. The doctor took him off steroids. She said the medicine had done its work. Simon was able to attend the Tigers' county championship game against the Ridgeway Hilltoppers. It was the first game he had seen Robbie play all season.

Robbie rose to the occasion. It was hard to imagine how he could have done any better than he had been doing all season. But he outdid himself this day.

The Hilltoppers had great fielding and good hitting. But their pitching staff was their weakness. Robbie didn't give the Ridgeway fielders much chance to show their stuff. His two home runs weren't long fly balls but screaming line drives. And his two doubles were just as solidly hit. All the Tigers played well in the 6–2 victory.

Robbie enjoyed going out with his parents after the game and celebrating. His mother talked about hitting, fielding, pitching, and the decisive plays in the game. His father's comments were more unusual. He talked about how the duel between pitcher and batter was like a showdown in a western movie. Simon praised Robbie for how he ran around the bases after his second home run. He liked the fact that Robbie did it humbly, not rubbing it in. Little details like this were what interested Simon.

The Riverton Tigers' first state regional play-off game was against the Grouton Leathernecks. Robbie had one of those days where he hit the ball as hard as he ever had—but right at the Grouton fielders. The game ended Robbie's hitting streak. He had no hits for the first time all season.

But the Tigers still scratched out an exciting 4–3 win. Ty went four for five, stole five bases, and scored three runs. He scored the winning run in the top of the ninth inning. He tagged up when Grouton's left fielder robbed Robbie of a home run.

Even though Robbie went hitless, scouts from everywhere pestered Coach Franklin for appointments to meet him. But now that Simon Belmont's vision problem seemed to be over, Robbie had no good reason to skip college. Coach Franklin turned all the pro scouts away, including Tilly Goodman from the L.A. Lions. But Tilly kept attending the Tigers' regional play-off games.

He wasn't going to let a prospect like Robbie get away so easily.

In a way, Robbie had warmed up to the idea of playing pro ball right after high school. When he thought of going to college next year, no real thrill of excitement came to him. He still hadn't decided yet between Lansley and Redstone. Ralph Butler gave a glowing report of Lansley University, so Robbie tended to favor it as his eventual choice. But he hadn't checked out its communications program yet.

Robbie also began nursing a secret desire. Maybe he would sign right into pro ball anyway, despite what his parents and coach wanted! He was eighteen now, old enough to make his own decisions.

Robbie knew Cynthia Wu would hate the idea, but she seemed to be out of his life now anyway. Dennis Wu said she and Eagle might attend the Tigers' next regional play-off game. Robbie found he was more concerned whether Tilly Goodman would be there. He wanted to impress the Lions' scout more than ever, hoping for an even bigger bonus offer. The June baseball draft was just a few weeks away.

"The Melinda problem" was also strong on his mind. Brian had finally gotten up enough nerve to tell Melinda how much he liked her. Melinda was very touched, but told Brian she liked him only as a friend. Brian told all this to Robbie later. Then Brian said something that really made Robbie's head spin.

"Melinda says she still likes Josh," Brian had said, "and maybe someone else, too. But she wouldn't say who it is."

Uh-oh, thought Robbie.

Riverton's opponent was the Prescott Hornets. Robbie was happy to spot Tilly Goodman's gold and brown cap in the bleachers behind home. The Tigers won a squeaker against Prescott. Robbie went one for five at the plate, tapping a single to left field for his only hit. His concentration was wavering again. And he couldn't blame Cynthia and Eagle, neither of whom made it to the game.

At the same time Robbie was faltering with his bat, his teammates' hitting picked up. It hadn't been all Belmont this season, and the rest of the Tiger team proved it. They never quit against Prescott, turning a 2–4 deficit into a 5–4 victory in the last two innings.

Robbie vowed he would redeem himself in the state championship game coming up. He did concentration exercises all week and took even more hitting practice. Melinda Clark asked him over to her house three times that week, but he only went once. They did nothing but watch video replays of Robbie's recent batting.

Robbie felt ready for baseball that Saturday. The game was being played in Municipal Stadium, home ballpark of the Brassville Bisons, a major-league team.

During batting practice before the game, the sound of the ball meeting Robbie's bat had never been louder. Tilly Goodman, Norman Taylor, Mack Doogan, and all the scouts as well as most of the ten thousand fans turned their heads when Robbie cracked out his hits.

"Way to sock 'em, Robbie!" called out Josh Kenny, sitting next to Melinda. Final exam week at Redstone University had ended the day before. Robbie knew Josh would be in the stands today. The chance of Riverton winning its second state baseball title in three years was too good for Josh to pass up.

"All right, all right, all right, all right!" called out Brian Webster from behind the batting cage. The sight of Melinda sitting next to Josh didn't make him cheery. But he was getting over his crush on her, and his old good humor was beginning to return.

Robbie didn't hear any cheers from the couple sitting behind Melinda and Joshua. It was Eagle Wilson, looking bored, and Cynthia Wu, looking shy. Robbie gave them a wave after his batting practice. Eagle half-waved, and Cynthia smiled nervously. *Real friendly couple*, Robbie thought. He felt a little bitter toward Cynthia. They hadn't talked since their fight. *Soon, I'll be playing baseball in Los Angeles*, he told himself, *so it doesn't matter*.

The sounds of Robbie's batting practice had excited everyone in the stadium. But now there was another, steady, repeating sound that got everyone's attention, including Robbie's. It was the sound of fast balls popping into a catcher's mitt. The pitcher for the other team, the Devon Wolverines, was warming up in the outfield bull-pen. The smack of his fast ball hitting leather echoed through the noisy stadium. It was the Wolverines' all-state pitcher, Ace Mahoney.

"I'll bet the catcher put shoe polish all over his glove to make that popping sound louder," Robbie said to Dennis Wu. "I hear they do that sometimes in pro ball."

"Maybe," said Dennis Wu, also watching Ace warm up in the distance. "Are my eyes tired or is that guy throwing the ball so fast I can hardly see it?"

Robbie squinted. *Those pitches sure do blur by*, he was thinking.

After the national anthem, the game began. Riverton was the "away" team for the game and batted first.

Ace Mahoney struck out Ty Williams, Abbie Jacobs, and Dennis Wu on nine pitches. It was an extraordinary way to open the championship. Players on Riverton's bench shook their heads in disbelief.

Robbie left the on-deck circle and put on his catcher's equipment. He was a little nervous about facing Ace Mahoney next inning. This was the first time he had felt nervous about facing a pitcher all year.

Wire had control trouble the first inning. The big crowd and the performance of Ace Mahoney had him rattled. It took a while before Robbie could settle Wire down. By that time, the

Wolverines had put two runs across the plate.

Robbie led off the top of the second inning. He had known about Ace's pitching skill before the game. The week before, Melinda had scouted the Wolverines. Her report said Ace threw a fast ball almost every pitch, with very good control. According to the report, Ace threw a curve or change-up only about once every five pitches. He didn't seem to care if the batter knew his fast ball was coming. He loved to overpower batters who thought they could hit fast balls. Melinda borrowed a radar gun from Coach Franklin and clocked Mahoney's fast ball. It came in at ninety miles per hour!

Robbie knew Mahoney had major-league speed, and he was eager to try his hand against it. If he was going to be a major leaguer soon, Robbie might as well get used to it. But he was nervous about facing it just the same.

Coach Franklin gave Robbie the sign to take the first pitch. Robbie was glad. He wanted to take a look at the fast ball he knew was coming.

On the mound, Ace Mahoney nodded at the catcher's signal. *One finger for a fast ball, no doubt*, thought Robbie. Ace stood six feet three inches tall and looked very strong. He had dark hair and a serious, respectful manner. His wind-up was smooth and steady. Robbie could see the power in Ace's body gather as the pitch lifted his left leg high. Then Ace rocked forward and fired.

The ball floated in at half speed. It was a change-up down the middle of the plate! Robbie watched with sharp regret as the fat pitch floated by. "Strike one!" called the umpire.

"Figured you'd want to take a look at his fast ball," said the Wolverine catcher, grinning. "Overrated, isn't it?"

Robbie stepped out of the batter's box. The slow pitch had been like a taunt from Mahoney. *Actually, it was the catcher who called the pitch,* thought Robbie. He knew how important a good catcher was to any good pitcher. It had been a smart call. It had taken Robbie's free view of the fast ball away from him.

Robbie stepped into the batter's box again. His palms were sweating. *Maybe that's why major leaguers wear batting gloves,* he thought. Mahoney went into his powerful wind-up again. *Here comes the speed!* thought Robbie.

And speed it had. As usual, Robbie fixed his gaze completely on the ball. His eyes said "swing!" and he swung.

Too late. The ball had already popped into the catcher's mitt with an ear-splitting sound. "Stee-rike two!" yelled the umpire.

"Tell me the truth, catch," said Robbie to Devon's catcher. "Do you put shoe polish on that mitt to make it pop louder?"

"No shoe polish, guy. But I do use four sponges in my mitt. My hand still swells up about the fourth inning."

I have to step before he releases the ball! Robbie told himself. This would be the first time Robbie had ever done that against a pitcher in organized baseball. And it had to be with the count 0–2 against him!

"You can do it, Robbie!" he heard Cynthia Wu's voice call out. A surge of confidence flooded through his body.

Mahoney wound up and heaved another smoker. Robbie stepped early, sensing Mahoney's rhythm. His eyes only had a split second to track the tiny white blur. His swing connected. *Wham!*

Riverton fans roared and jumped to their feet. The ball disappeared over the left-field wall— but on the wrong side of the foul pole. The Tiger fans moaned, then started lightly applauding the power behind the well-hit foul ball. Despite Mahoney's blazing speed, Robbie had got around on the ball too early!

Ace Mahoney gave Robbie a cold look. Devon's catcher said, "Beginner's luck, guy."

"You wish," said Robbie back, with a tight smile. *I can hit this guy!* he told himself. He stepped into the box with renewed confidence.

Robbie ran the count to 2–2. Then he tagged the next pitch, another Mahoney monster fast ball, deep into left-center field. But Robbie got a bit under the ball, which was caught on the warning track. It was a long, high out.

Robbie was the only Tiger who could get good wood on the ball against Mahoney. Even Ty Williams kept whiffing at the plate. Like Robbie, Ty hadn't struck out all season before this game.

Mahoney had six no-hitters among the dozen victories he piled up this past season. More and more, it looked like the state final would be his seventh no-hitter and "lucky thirteenth" win.

Wire seemed to pick up inspiration from Ace Mahoney's pitching. After the first inning, he handled the Wolverine batters much better. Hitting wasn't Devon's strong point anyway. It was pitching—and mainly Ace Mahoney. He had brought the Wolverines this far, and he was the one keeping them ahead now.

The game rolled quickly into the fifth inning without further scoring. Robbie popped up his second time at bat. But he hit a rare Mahoney curve ball for a one-out single in the eighth inning, ruining Ace's no-hitter. Clearly upset with himself, Mahoney then walked Eddie Mosely and Sam Thorne, loading the bases. Devon's catcher walked out to the mound and had a few words with his pitcher. Ace then bore down again, striking out Todd Murphy and Cat Malone on six straight pitches to end the inning.

The score still hadn't changed from the first inning. It was 2–0, Devon. Ned Burney came in to relieve an arm-weary Wire in the eighth and struck out the side. The Tigers had their last chance in the top of the ninth inning. Robbie didn't know if he'd get another at-bat or not. He was slated to bat fifth this last inning.

Freshman catcher Guy Henry hadn't seen much game action this past season. But he always gave his best, and lately he had been making good contact with the bat in practice. Coach

Franklin told him to pinch-hit for Ned Burney to start off the ninth inning.

The speed of the first Mahoney fast ball thrown to Guy caught him flat-footed. But he took good cuts at the next two pitches, both smokers as before. Mahoney overwhelmed him, however, sending Guy down on strikes. Even from the dugout steps, Robbie could see that Mahoney's fast ball was gaining, not losing, speed now. The Devon pitcher obviously wanted to close the game out as quickly as possible.

But Ace's control as he threw harder started to become sloppy. Ty finally avoided striking out by drawing a walk. He trotted down to first base clapping his hands. Abbie Jacobs ticked a weak ground ball to third. Devon's third baseman fielded it and got the force-out at second. But Abbie Jacobs beat the throw to first. Then Dennis Wu took four straight high balls.

Robbie Belmont was up with runners on first and second base. He represented the go-ahead, possibly winning run.

Chapter Twelve

Robbie stepped into the batter's box. Ace Mahoney didn't look cool, calm, and collected anymore. Robbie could see the sweat on his forehead. Ace was breathing faster. He went into his stretch, then checked his runners. The fast ball he threw was clocked at a dizzying ninety-one miles per hour.

Overall, this was the fifteenth Mahoney fast ball thrown to Robbie in the game. But its speed still surprised him. He fouled a zinger into the first-base stands. A group of fans jumped out of the ball's way. Strike one.

Robbie didn't expect Mahoney to throw him any more curves since he had hit one for a single earlier. But the next pitch was a curve—a good one. It caught Robbie off guard. He swung and missed. "Strike two!" called the umpire.

The Devon catcher snapped the ball back to the pitcher. Ace took off his cap and wiped his forehead with his sleeve. Robbie moved closer to the plate. He still wanted to swing for a home run. That seemed to be the Tigers' best chance to win the game. But with two strikes and no balls, he couldn't wait for the perfect home-run pitch any longer. He had to swing at anything near the strike zone.

Mahoney looked in for the catcher's signal. He shook his head—he wanted another signal. Then he shook off the second signal. At this point, Robbie stepped out of the batter's box.

Why did he shake off two signals? Robbie wondered. *The first was probably a fast ball. That means the second was probably a curve or a change-up. So are we back to a fast ball? Devon's catcher is no dummy. Something's up. But what?*

"Time, ump," shouted the Wolverines' catcher now. He went out to the mound. Ace Mahoney said two words to him. The catcher nodded and ran back behind the plate.

Robbie stepped back into the box. He was ready for anything, but he was expecting a waste pitch. What Ace had said to his catcher had sounded a little like "fishball."

Ace threw the next pitch overhanded. It came in fast but not as fast as usual. It looked like it might go a little inside. *Too fast for a curve!* Robbie thought. He was just about to check his swing and let the ball pass inside. But it was too close to the strike zone. *Have to swing!* Robbie's wrists continued turning.

Suddenly, the ball fell straight down. It dropped

as if an invisible rope had yanked it from below. Robbie couldn't adjust his swing in time.

"Stee-rike three!" came the plate umpire's chilling call.

The word "three" was barely out of the plate umpire's mouth when the Wolverine catcher rushed toward Mahoney and jumped on him. The rest of the Devon team ran over and joined their two teammates on the mound. There were high fives, back slaps, handshakes, tossed caps, pats, hugs, and shouts of joy among all the Wolverines now. And many of their fans spilled out of the stands and onto the field, whooping and clapping. The Devon Wolverines had beaten the Riverton Tigers, 2–0, for the state title!

Robbie Belmont recalled the first time he had ever struck out as a Riverton Tiger. It had happened during his first at-bat in his first game as a freshman. Now, in his last time up ever for the Tigers, he had struck out again. And it couldn't have come at a worse time.

Retreating in stunned silence to the dugout, Robbie was clapped on the shoulder by Dennis Wu. "Rough luck, Robbie."

"Mahoney threw me a split-fingered fast ball. I didn't even know he *had* a splitter," said Robbie glumly.

"What was that?" asked Coach Franklin. "He threw you a spitter?"

"No, Coach," said Robbie. "A split-fingered fast ball. First time I saw it today."

"First time anyone's seen it, probably," said

131

the coach. "He was saving it for a special occasion, and you just happened to be the occasion, Robbie. It happens."

The Wolverines finally untangled themselves. They came over and shook hands with the Tiger players.

"Good game."

"Nice game."

"Great game."

"Nice single."

"Thanks. Good game."

Robbie shook the hands stretched toward him and kept his voice steady. He felt dazed and stupid. Finally, he shook hands with Ace Mahoney. "Where've you been hiding that splitter?" Robbie asked him.

"Secret weapon," said Ace.

"Thought so," said Robbie.

There was a pause.

"I'll tell you something, Belmont. I wouldn't have used it at all if I didn't think I needed it against you. I wanted to go with just heat, but my catcher thought you might get around on it. I have my catcher to thank for the call."

Robbie grunted a laugh. "Figures I'd be outfoxed by a fellow catcher. Just the same, *you* were the one who threw the pitch. I just hope I get another crack at you sometime down the road."

"Maybe. You never know."

"Yeah. Great game, Ace," said Robbie, shaking his hand again.

"Good try, Belmont," said Ace, turning for the locker room.

Robbie watched him go. He felt as if he were standing in wet cement.

There were only a few more weeks of school left. Graduation was approaching. And so was June fifth, the day the major-league baseball draft began.

But all Robbie could think about was striking out against Ace Mahoney. He knew he shouldn't brood about it. But he still couldn't get it out of his mind.

He kept going over each pitch of the strikeout, wondering what he could have done differently. He thought he should have seen it coming. He should have expected a new pitch after Ace had shaken off two signals and had a conference with his catcher.

Robbie watched Melinda's videocassette of the game and strikeout over and over, a couple of times a week. Melinda stopped watching it with him after seeing it once. She and Joshua, who was back from college for the summer, were on really good terms again. She and Robbie went back to the brother-sister relationship they had before.

Melinda decided to attend Whalen University in the fall. Everyone agreed it was the best choice, especially Joshua. Robbie still hadn't bothered to choose between Lansley and Redstone. He was secretly planning to accept Tilly Goodman's bonus offer of what he hoped would be one hundred thousand dollars.

The doctor had finally made a diagnosis regarding Simon Belmont. "She said I had 'possible MS,'" Simon told Robbie. Ellen Belmont, Robbie's mother, was sitting quietly and listening. "That means the lab tests didn't really prove it was multiple sclerosis. But there are other signs it is. MS attacks can come and go. If I do have it, I could have another vision attack some time in the future. It could be two years or twenty. I did have a spell of blurry vision when I was twenty-five. It only lasted ten minutes, and I forgot about it. That could have been my first MS attack, though."

"Isn't there any way to find out for sure whether you have it or not?" Robbie asked.

"There's one test I haven't had yet," answered Simon. "But it costs an awful lot of money."

"Well, you should take it, no matter what the cost!" Robbie was surprised at how firmly he said this.

"I agree with Robbie, Simon," said Ellen Belmont now. "You should take the test. To be sure."

"I will if I absolutely have to," said Simon Belmont stubbornly. "But let's wait awhile. Let's give the doctor a chance to see if it's MS without my having to take the test."

Robbie looked at his mother. *She's thinking what I'm thinking—it's the money that's holding him back!*

*   *   *

On the morning of June sixth, two days after graduation, Robbie waited anxiously for the mailman. The baseball draft had begun the day before. Major-league teams usually informed draft prospects of the results by phone call or overnight mail. Robbie had not received a phone call yet.

Simon and Ellen Belmont didn't even know their son was waiting for the draft results. They thought he was still planning to go to college but hadn't yet decided where. Robbie hadn't told them of his plan to play pro ball right out of high school.

At eleven o'clock that morning, Robbie heard the mailman pushing the mail through the front-door slot. He hurried to get it. He spotted the overnight mail envelope right away. Robbie picked it up and tore it open.

It was a formal letter on official Los Angeles Lions' stationery. It informed Robbie that the Lions were willing to sign him for . . . twenty thousand dollars.

Twenty thousand? Robbie cried to himself. *What happened to one hundred thousand?*

There was also a personal note from Tilly Goodman in the envelope. It read as follows:

Dear Robbie,

That last game against Ace Mahoney hurt, obviously. I had to include it in my scouting report, just as I included all the good things you did all year through. And there were a lot of those!

But the front office had second thoughts about you. It doesn't like its draftees to struggle against high-school pitching, especially in the clutch. Mahoney has major-league speed, which made the front office even more reluctant to draft you higher. They felt if you had struggled then, what would happen later?

Don't be discouraged, though. The Lions still want you in their organization. That's why they picked you on the nineteenth round. The twenty thousand dollars is in addition to the college plan we'd put you on. Hope you take it. We have fifteen days to hammer out a contract. Let me know what you decide. Either way, you're still a heckuva prospect!

Regards,
Tilly Goodman

Robbie crumpled both letters in his hands. He had made up his mind—college. But which one?

A week passed. Robbie would start his summer job doing construction work in a short while. The days were long and boring to him. Then one morning, he received another piece of mail. Robbie nearly jumped when he saw the name handwritten over the return address. It was from Eddie Trent!

Robbie had been glad that Eddie hadn't seen

the state final against the Wolverines. *But what could he possibly be writing me about now? A consolation letter?*

Robbie opened the letter slowly, then brightened as he read it. Eddie was inviting him to play in a high-school all-star game. It was called the "Johnston Senior All-American Game." And it was to take place next week! Eddie Trent was one of the two major-league players who would help coach the teams. The manager of one of the teams would be Frank Preston from Redstone University.

Eddie added a few personal remarks as well: "I heard about Riverton's loss in the state championship. I also heard you had a tough day at the plate. Hang tough! I have a feeling this game may make you feel a little better."

A full roster of players was enclosed. Robbie felt a sharp stab of excitement when he recognized two names. They were listed under the team that would oppose Robbie's.

Ace Mahoney and Jason Jackson.

Chapter Thirteen

The minor-league ballpark in Johnston was filled to capacity for the game. The best graduating high-school baseball players in the country were all in one place! Scouts from every major-league team were in the stands. There were scouts in sweat shirts and scouts in three-piece suits. They occupied the lower sections of the stands. Friends of the players and just fans of baseball from miles around crammed the stadium this day. Not one seat was empty.

About fifty Riverton fans had made the trip. Robbie's parents took a short vacation to be there. They drove with Brian and Robbie to Johnston. Simon Belmont was happy to do most of the driving.

Gus Franklin had come by plane with his wife, Carol. She was a judge for the state court, but you couldn't tell from how she acted today. "Hey, Robbie baby!" Carol Franklin yelled to him from her seat by the dugout. "Nice uniform! Best on the field!" The Franklins were sitting next to New York Titans' scout Mack Doogan.

Melinda Clark had wanted to come. But she decided to stay behind with Joshua, who was celebrating his birthday.

Robbie was already waiting for his turn in the batting cage. He was swinging his favorite black bat, the one his dad bought for him. Robbie made sure it traveled with them in the car. He refused to put it in the trunk for fear it would get nicked or chipped somehow. The bat was in his lap the whole trip.

The uniforms on the all-stars were different styles and colors, reflecting the different high schools they represented. Robbie's was white with orange. Ace Mahoney's Wolverine uniform was white with brown pinstripes. The hulk who was catching Ace wore a gray uniform with red sleeves and socks. That was Jason Jackson, from an Oklahoma team called the Chickaw Red Hens. He was *huge*.

Eddie Trent was wearing his familiar blue and orange New York Titans' uniform. It had the number 8 on the back, same as Robbie's. Eddie was talking with Frank Preston, the manager of Robbie's team, the East team. Frank wore the uniform of the Redstone University Colts: red, with just a few brown markings.

The major-league star who was coaching the West team was Scott Newhouse, slugger for the Los Angeles Lions. He was now talking with the manager of the West team, George Harrington, head baseball coach of the Lansley University Jets.

The brown and gold cap worn by Newhouse reminded Robbie of L. A. Lions' scout Tilly Goodman. Tilly, of course, was here today as well. One part of Tilly's note still bothered Robbie: The front office "doesn't like its draftees to struggle against high-school pitching, especially in the clutch." Tilly had called Robbie a few days after sending the letter. Robbie had politely said, "No thanks, Mr. Goodman. I'm going to college." They hadn't communicated with each other since.

Both Eddie Trent and Scott Newhouse had a couple of days off before their next major-league game. That's why they could make the game today in Johnston. Besides, each enjoyed helping out the talented high-school players now loosening up on the field.

Eddie Trent was still talking with Frank Preston near the third-base line when Eddie waved Robbie over. Robbie hustled to where the two coaches were standing.

"Have you caught your pitchers yet, Robbie?" Eddie asked.

"Yes. They're quite a group. All good, but different!" said Robbie.

"You've batted against one of the other team's pitchers, right?" Frank Preston asked him.

"Yes, sir, I have. Ace Mahoney."

"What's he got?"

"Well, the ninety-mile fast ball is his main

pitch. It comes in fast and with some movement, a little lift. He doesn't use his curve much. It's good, but hittable. He has an average change-up. And he threw me a split-fingered fast ball once. It was the only time in the game that he used it. It was a very tough pitch—he should use it more. He might tip it off, though, by throwing it more overhand than his other pitches."

"Hmm. Thanks, Robbie. I think it's your turn in the batting cage."

Robbie walked back to home plate and started taking his batting cuts. His hitting turned quite a few heads in the stadium. With ten swings, he parked three home runs, three off the wall, and four line drives. There was scattered applause from the stands.

"Way to rip, kid!" said Eddie, giving Robbie a pat on the back.

"Thanks, Eddie," said Robbie. "Can I ask you something?"

"Shoot."

"How come Ace Mahoney and I are on different teams? I mean, we're from the same state."

"Well, as I understand it," Eddie replied, "the scouts voted for more players from the east than the west this year. Of course, I did have a *small* part in how the teams were divided, but not much." He smiled at Robbie.

Robbie grinned back. "Well, whatever you did, I'm sure it was fair. Thanks for inviting me."

"I sent the letter of invitation, Robbie, but it was the scouts who voted you in. If you want to thank *me*, however, do it with your bat today. Mind if I take a look at it?"

"No, not at all," said Robbie, handing his bat to him. Eddie took some smooth practice swings with it. It was amazing how such an easy swing could look so powerful.

"That's a beauty, Robbie," said Eddie, handing back the bat. "There's a lot of hits in it, I can tell."

At this point, Robbie looked across the field and saw Scott Newhouse talking with Jason Jackson.

"That Jackson is one big catcher," Robbie said.

"True," said Eddie. "And Scott, I'm sure, is doing what he can to see that Jason signs with the Lions. Tilly Goodman offered Jason a huge bonus, I hear."

"What?" blurted Robbie in shock. He couldn't believe it. "How much?"

"I usually don't talk about this sort of thing, Robbie. Professional habit and all. But the number I heard was a hundred thousand."

"A hundred thousand!" Robbie lowered his voice when he saw some of his teammates turn their heads toward him. "That's the same amount I"—Robbie checked himself here—"that's quite a bit of money! He must be really good!" Robbie was thinking of *Fisk & Foster* magazine. It had rated Jackson the top high-school prospect in the country this year.

"He is," said Eddie, "but not as good as you."

The vote of confidence from Eddie Trent gave Robbie a boost. They stood and watched Jason Jackson take some batting practice. He had a big, powerful swing. Still, he didn't connect solidly with the ball all the time, even in batting practice. But when he did connect, the ball exploded out of the park.

"He's also a pretty nimble catcher, despite his size," said Eddie. "But he has a chip on his shoulder for some reason. And he doesn't think ahead as well as you do, Robbie. Remember that."

Robbie's team was simply called the East. The other team was called the West. The East took the field first, with Robbie as starting catcher.

The first pitcher he caught was a rangy, two-hundred-pound player named Tex Madden. Tex was a friendly sort, but on the mound he was all business. Tex threw faster than Wire, but not as fast as Ace Mahoney.

Tex had a curve ball, however, that almost made Robbie laugh in disbelief. He aimed it about two feet behind a right-handed batter. Then it broke four or five feet! It was as if some unseen tennis player suddenly whacked the pitch in a different direction once it got close to the batter.

In the beginning, Robbie had felt a little awkward meeting so many new players. Everyone felt a little nervous about getting along with so many strangers. But Tex had made friends with Robbie early. This made Robbie feel much more at ease on the East team.

The first batter had a yellow and black uniform on. His name was lettered across the back of his uniform. But it had so many letters it barely fit across his wide shoulders. And what a name it was: Anthony Sciannimanico!

The crowd laughed when the public-address announcer tried to say Anthony's last name.

"How do you pronounce that last name?" Robbie asked.

"You don't pronounce it—you sing it," the dark-haired youth said. He flashed a smile, then stepped into the box.

Tex threw two fast balls to bring the count to 1–1. Robbie then called for a curve ball. He was almost grinning in anticipation. The fabulous Tex curve came in. When it started behind Anthony, he lurched forward. Then it curved, and Anthony lurched backward! The ball angled sharply across the outside corner. "Strike two!" called the umpire.

Anthony Sciannimanico stepped out of the box. "Man, that was some curve!" he said in admiration. Robbie had to laugh. The crowd loved it. Players from both teams were smiling.

Tex ran the count to 3–2 before Robbie called for the curve again. It was just as spectacular as the first curve, with one difference. Anthony Sciannimanico proved why his all-star credentials were as long as his name. Without flinching, he hung in and lined the veering pitch right down the first-base line.

It looked like a sure double, maybe a triple.

144

But suddenly, the East's first baseman, Tim Rifkin, dove five feet and knocked the ball down. The flip to Tex Madden covering the bag was close. But Anthony Sciannimanico had great speed and beat it by a hair. It was an infield single.

The all-stars might be playing for fun, but they were also playing hard.

Robbie could tell Anthony wanted to steal. He took a long lead, and he was leaning toward second ever so slightly. But Anthony didn't break for second on the first pitch, a fast-ball strike. Without hesitation, Robbie pegged the ball down to Rifkin at first. It was a perfect throw, and Anthony was a little too casual getting back to the bag. In a very close play, the umpire called Anthony out!

A long argument followed. It was still a friendly game, but it was also heating up. Everybody wanted to do well—and win.

"Way to look, Belmont!" Frank Preston's voice called out. Robbie could also hear Brian Webster and the other Riverton fans screaming their approval. The crowd applauded the pick-off throw. The scouts didn't applaud. They just clicked their stopwatches and scribbled in their notebooks.

Tex Madden's speed and amazing curve retired the next two West batters easily. It was the East team's turn to bat.

Ace Mahoney did not start for the West. Each team had three pitchers, who would pitch three innings apiece. The West's first pitcher was Darryl "Duke" Jamison. Duke was what the scouts called a "small righty." Usually, small right-handed pitchers were not considered good prospects for the major leagues, no matter how well they threw. But Duke had something that made the scouts vote him into this game. It was also rumored among the players that Duke had received a high five-figure bonus to sign with the Dallas Stallions.

What Darryl Jamison had was extraordinary control. He could throw a baseball precisely where he wanted. Duke struck out the East side with corner-nicking sliders and kneecap fast balls. Robbie was batting fifth in the order. He didn't get a chance to taste Duke's servings in the first inning.

The first West batter up in the top of the second inning was catcher Jason Jackson. He stood six feet five inches tall and weighed a rock-solid 275 pounds. Robbie remembered that Jackson didn't hit the ball consistently. So Robbie called mostly for Tex's curve. After booming two mighty fouls, Jason finally popped one straight up in the air.

"Home run in an elevator shaft" is what players called this kind of pop-up. The crowd gasped and oohed as the ball shot straight up and kept climbing.

Robbie looked up for the tiny dot in the blue sky. But the sun blinded him. He put his glove up to block the glare. Little bright, round white lights were dancing before his eyes. Still, he was drifting under the ball. He let himself keep drifting. He remembered what he had learned during those drills Coach Franklin put him through in the rain.

The sparkling dots before his eyes started to fade. He could now see the ball falling. Robbie ran toward the West team's dugout. The West players were screaming at him.

"Watch out for the steps, guy!"

"Hey, Belmont! Your pants are falling down!"

"Yo, catch, aren't you Bob Hope's brother? No Hope!"

"Don't flub it, Belmont! *Thousands* are watching you!"

But Robbie felt confident. He kept watching the ball and settled under it nicely. After a short wait, the ball plunked into his mitt. *Just another out!* he thought. But he had never seen a ball hit so high!

Tex Madden managed to retire the side without allowing any runs.

The East's cleanup batter ahead of Robbie was a tall right fielder named Strom Farrell. Strom had the build of a power forward on a pro basketball team. His swing was smooth as silk. He swung at a bad pitch, high and outside. But he stroked it on the fat of the bat. The ball rocketed against the right-field wall for a standup double.

"So you're Belmont," Jason Jackson said as Robbie stepped into the batter's box. "You don't look like much. Can't figure why the scouts would have rated you second to me as a catcher, you know? I would have rated you a *lot* lower."

Robbie stepped out of the box.

"Hoo-boy!" said Jackson, chuckling. "A sensitive type!"

"Put a cork in it, catcher," said the plate umpire.

"No rule against me talking, ump," said Jackson. "Get in there and bat, Belmont, if you want to call it batting."

Robbie didn't move. The manager for the West team called out, "Make him quit stalling, ump!" When Robbie glanced over, George Harrington was pointing at him.

Harrington had said a few words to Robbie before the game. George had seemed happy that Robbie was interested in Lansley. But he also acted as if there was no question which college Robbie would choose.

East manager Frank Preston climbed out of the dugout. He called over to George, "Tell your catcher to stop yakking so much, George, or I won't send you a Christmas card this year!"

There was a pause. Then George Harrington laughed. "You're right, Frank. Jackson, knock it off back there!"

"Okay, Coach," Jackson said in a voice only Robbie could hear. "No need for a psych job on Mr. Strikeout King anyway."

"Thanks, Mr. Pop-up!" Robbie couldn't help saying. He stepped back into the box.

Robbie let the first pitch by Darryl Jamison

go by for a called ball. Jackson caught the pitch and immediately threw the ball to second! Strom Farrell, trying to steal, dove for the bag. But Jackson's peg was perfect. Strom was tagged out. The crowd applauded.

"Anybody can pick people off at first," Jason said. "Second is harder."

"Nice throw," Robbie admitted.

As Duke's next pitch curved in toward the low inside corner, Robbie heard Jackson mutter, "Take a poke at that, Mr. Fifth-in-the-Order!"

But the pitch was coming into Robbie's favorite homer zone, low and inside! He waited just long enough to get a good look at the ball. Then he swung.

Robbie knew it was a home run the moment he hit it. The ball sailed high into the left-field stands. The crowd roared. It was the first score in the game.

As Robbie crossed home plate, Jason Jackson gave him a menacing stare.

Chapter Fourteen

The score stayed 1–0 until the top of the fourth inning. Tex Madden had held the West team to two hits and gave up two walks in three innings. Two runners tried to steal on Robbie. He threw them both out.

Jason Jackson also threw out two more base runners trying to steal. The fans were getting interested in the duel between Jason and Robbie, and so were the scouts.

The second time Jackson batted was against the East team's second pitcher, Bart Nuxley. Bart was nicknamed Nux, not just because of his last name. His best pitch was a knuckle ball. It broke crazily each time. Nux threw the pitch hard, too.

Robbie had never caught a knuckle-ball pitcher before. He never knew which way the ball would break. The first pitch to Jackson broke to the right and bit the dirt. Jackson took a big swing at it and missed. Robbie had to throw his body at the pitch to stop it.

150

Nux's next pitch fluttered in. Robbie waited for it to dart or break, but it just hung in the air. This was one knuckle ball that didn't do anything. Jackson got all of it, pummeling it high over the center-field wall.

The West team's catcher trotted around the bases with both fists in the air, drinking in the crowd's cheers. Robbie was impressed by the distance of the hit, but not with the fact that the ball *was* hit. The pitch had been the fattest gopher ball Robbie could imagine.

The score was 1–1 when the East team batted next. The West team's second pitcher liked to throw breaking balls. His name was Byron Maddox. He threw not only plenty of knuckle balls, but also a fork ball. Some of the East batters thought it was a spitball. Strom Farrell swung at and missed a pitch that slipped under his bat at the last instant. He asked the plate umpire to check the ball.

But Jackson dropped the ball into the dirt and fumbled with it there before picking it up. When the umpire finally got a look at it, he found no wetness on it.

Jackson was putting on an impressive catching performance. Many of Maddox's pitches were wild, but Jackson still blocked them. The West catcher had surprisingly quick hands and feet for someone of his size. The fans cheered his blocked pitches just as loudly as they had when Robbie blocked Nux's knuckle balls.

Strom Farrell finally topped a sinker. Jackson

leapt out of his catcher's box and pounced on the dribbler. He managed to throw Strom out by a hair at first. Tim Rifkin, who was on first, went to second on the infield out.

Now it was Robbie's turn to take a look at Byron Maddox's breaking pitches. Robbie worked the count to 2–2. The next pitch dipped sharply for ball three. Robbie asked the umpire to look the ball over. But Jason Jackson had already dropped and dribbled the ball into the dirt.

"Don't touch it, catcher," said the plate umpire quickly. The umpire stooped over and picked the ball up. Once again, there was no way of knowing if it had any "unnatural" moisture on it. The umpire put the ball into his pocket and threw out a new one to the pitcher. Then he said to Jackson, "There will be no more dropped balls into the dirt, catcher. Am I understood?" Jackson nodded.

Robbie didn't get any more pitches that looked like spitballs that time up. Maddox instead tried sneaking a fast ball by him. Robbie socked it for a clean single up the middle. Strom Farrell's long legs brought him quickly to home. As Strom approached, Jason Jackson blocked the plate. The big catcher acted as if the ball were coming in for a close play at home, even though it wasn't. Strom slid in a cloud of dust. Jason backed away at the last second, laughing.

Robbie stayed on first, happy to have knocked in the go-ahead run. He was also eager to try his hand at stealing second against Jackson. Robbie's daring lead made Byron throw to first base a few times. This helped Robbie learn how Maddox's back heel moved when he threw to first and home.

Finally, with the count 2–2, Robbie was ready to take off. He felt he could get the best possible jump on Maddox now. If Byron threw another dipsy-doodle pitch, that would give Robbie even more time to beat the throw.

Robbie had never wanted to steal as much as he did now. He took a long lead, but not long enough to make Maddox throw to first. Byron went into his stretch. He looked over his shoulder at Robbie. He seemed to wait a long time, then stepped off the rubber. Robbie hustled back to first.

Maddox toed the rubber again. Robbie took a good lead again. Byron didn't peer over at first base for long this time. He hoped his quick move to home plate would surprise Robbie. But Robbie had his eyes on the pitcher's back heel. When Maddox made his move to the plate, Robbie was already off and running.

He ran with his head down the first half of the distance. Robbie did not look back to see where the ball was. He didn't want to waste a moment of energy. Robbie saw by the second baseman's position that the peg would be almost exactly on the bag. All Robbie could do was run as fast as he could, then slide as best as he could. His trailing leg hooked the inside corner of the bag. "Safe!" called the umpire on the play. Both the second baseman and the shortstop complained to the umpire, but it was to no avail. The crowd gave Robbie a big round of applause. It was the first stolen base of the day!

But Robbie was left stranded on second as Maddox bore down and retired the rest of the side.

The first four innings had featured all-star pitching. In the fifth and sixth innings, all-star hitting stole the show. Bart Nuxley and Byron Maddox were both shelled heavily. Players who had hit for a high average during the regular season now showed their stuff. Robbie felt proud to be among such company. The sound of ball meeting bat was like a drum track keeping time during these innings. Robbie and Jackson each added a double to their output. When the dust had settled after the bottom of the sixth inning, the score was 6–5 in favor of the West.

Then the strongest pitcher on each all-star team came in. Very quickly, the hot hitting became cold.

The new pitcher for the East team was Roger Boyce, a pale, freckled, red-headed giant from Georgia. Robbie loved how Roger pitched. He looked as mild as milk when he took the signal and wound up. But right before his release, he seemed to turn into a furious bull.

Boyce's fast ball impressed the scouts holding radar guns—ninety miles per hour. It also had good motion that led to a lot of missed swings and pop-ups. And Boyce had a really good curve ball. It didn't break as much as Tex Madden's, but it was fast and darting, with a tight spin. With no trouble, Roger Boyce struck out the first batter. The second batter flied out to short left field. The third batter, Ace Mahoney, took three called strikes in a row.

Ace Mahoney, however, was up to the challenge. He only had to throw five pitches to retire the East hitters in the bottom of the seventh inning. Frank Preston had told his team what Robbie had said about Ace's pitching. But the first two batters hit easy grounders back to the pitcher. The third batter sliced a blooper to short right field that looked as if it might fall in. But Anthony Sciannimanico made a flying, skidding grab of it. The crowd buzzed about the catch during the change of inning.

Roger Boyce gave up his first hit, a single, to the West team's first batter in the top of the eighth inning. Robbie called for Boyce's sinking curve ball to the next batter. The batter swung, knocking the pitch to the shortstop. He tossed the ball to the second baseman, who tossed it to first for the double play.

The third West batter this inning tapped an easy two-hopper to Tim Rifkin at first base. The side was out.

Robbie Belmont's return match with Ace Mahoney would be in the bottom of the eighth inning. He was scheduled to bat second, and he was looking forward to it.

Robbie had reminded Strom Farrell about Ace's

split-fingered fast ball right before Strom went to the plate. "Remember," said Robbie, "if he throws it straight overhand, that's the tip-off."

The first three pitches to Strom were all fast balls, two going for strikes. Then, with the count at 1–2, Ace came straight overhand with his next pitch. Strom slammed it past Ace's ear for a hard single.

"All right, Strom!" Robbie yelled. He walked up to the plate and dug in. *Hmm*, thought Robbie, *this is a familiar situation*. Once again, he represented the go-ahead, possibly winning run. And once again, Mahoney was all that could stop him from getting it.

Ace looked in for Jason Jackson's signal. Ace and Robbie had only said a few words to each other during the pregame warm-ups. It was as if they both knew their main encounter would be on the diamond. And here it was. Ace showed no sign of recognizing Robbie. He was all business, and the business was serious.

"Come on, Robbie!" he heard Eddie Trent's voice call out. "Show this guy where you live!"

Ace's first pitch was his thundering fast ball. Frank Preston had given Robbie the take sign for the first pitch. So Robbie let the fast ball zip by without swinging. "Stee-rike one!" yelled the plate umpire.

The scouts' radar guns registered ninety-two miles per hour. Some of the scouts leaned over and looked at the others' radar guns to be sure they clocked the pitch correctly. Each had ninety-two showing in red numerals.

Jason Jackson was delighted. "Someone nail that piece of lumber to your shoulder, Belmont?" He clucked his tongue as he threw the ball back to Mahoney on the mound.

Robbie said nothing. He was deep in concentration, watching the ball in Ace's hand.

Mahoney threw the next pitch straight overhand! *Aha! Split-fingered fast ball!* thought Robbie as the ball shot in. He started his swing, waiting for the ball to break. But it never did. His swing was late, and he missed the ball completely.

"Guess you thought Ace there never threw a regular overhand fast ball," said Jackson. His voice was loud enough for the East team's dugout to hear.

Smart pitch, Robbie thought in grudging admiration.

Ace wasted the next two pitches, running the count to 2–2. He seemed to reach back for a little more on his next pitch. And he threw it overhand! Robbie had to be ready for either the split-fingered or regular fast ball now. He focused all his attention on the ball. Jackson was babbling something to try to distract Robbie, but Robbie barely heard it. Then the pitch dipped sharply! It *was* the splitter!

Robbie had seen this pitch a thousand times in his head. He had gone over it inch by inch, remembering every detail. At night, trying to sleep, he would pretend it was coming toward him right there in bed. He had memorized how the ball would suddenly dip.

The splitter heading for him now wasn't exactly the same. But it wasn't all that different, either. Robbie's eyes grew wider as they fixed on the sinking pitch. Swinging at this pitch was like coming home for Robbie.

The crunch of the black marbled bat hitting the ball felt terrific to Robbie. The ball rose on a 45-degree angle. It kept rising until some eleven-year-old girl with a mitt caught it in the top row of the bleachers beyond the left-field wall. It was a two-run homer—off Ace Mahoney!

Robbie jogged out the homer in his usual unflashy way. But inside, he felt as if he were running on air.

The cheering and clapping were still going on as Robbie entered the dugout. There, he allowed himself the luxury of grinning. *Ah!* was what he kept thinking to himself. The score was 7–6, East team.

The next batter for the East hit a towering pop-up toward the West team's dugout. Jason Jackson raced to get under it, then fell into the dugout! The ball was going to come down safely. But at the last second, the West catcher lunged out of the dugout and snagged the ball. It was caught well in front of the dugout.

The crowd loved it. Jackson held the ball over his head and bowed! The cheering got louder.

Eddie Trent shook his head. "It's one thing to make a hard catch look easy—quite another to make an easy catch look hard. That whole show was unnecessary. And reckless."

"The guy's a showboat," said Bert Nagata, the small but speedy third baseman for the East. "Robbie's better."

"Thanks, Bert!" said Robbie.

The next East batter ripped a Mahoney curve ball for a triple. Suddenly, the all-star hitting was catching up with the all-star pitching again. But the next East batter hit the ball a couple of inches in front of home plate.

Cat-quick, Jason Jackson pounced on the ball and tagged the startled batter out. The tag seemed more aggressive than it needed to be. The runner on third had run for home when the bat ticked the ball. But when he saw the batter get tagged, the runner stopped, turned, and started running back to third.

Jackson ran after him at full throttle. He could have tossed it to the West third baseman for an easy out. But Jackson seemed determined to make the play himself. He finally caught the runner and tagged him hard on the head. The runner winced and yelled at Jackson for tagging him so hard. Jackson just spit in the dirt and stood there.

Fans for the West team cheered for Jackson's unassisted double play. He lifted both hands over his head.

"That clown thinks he's winning the game all by himself," said Robbie, putting his shin guards on. "And he tags a little too hard for my taste."

159

"My taste, too," said Frank Preston.

Robbie looked up, surprised. He didn't know anyone had been listening to him just then.

"Forget about Jackson, Robbie," added Preston. "You're playing a whale of a game." The remark made Robbie feel better as he headed out of the dugout for the top of the ninth inning.

Jason Jackson led off for the West team. Fans of the West team gave him a big hand. But Robbie heard Carol Franklin's voice ring out loud and clear, "Blow this hot-dog away, East!" Gus Franklin seemed to slouch down after his wife said this.

Roger Boyce threw a curve ball in tight to Jackson. The West catcher hit it off his handle for a cracked-bat single to left field. A bit rattled by the hit, Roger walked the next West batter. Now the West had men on first and second base with no outs.

With the count 2–1 on the next batter, the base runners took off on the next pitch. It was a hit-and-run play! The batter hit a hard two-hopper over the third-base bag. In a flash, Bert Nagata backhanded it. Bert had a force chance at every base.

But Jason Jackson, all 275 pounds of him, had been running hard with the pitch. He barreled into the small third baseman, who was sent flying backward. The ball jiggled out of Bert's hand in the process. The bases were now loaded. There were no outs.

Bert Nagata called time to walk off the wooziness he was feeling. Jason Jackson stood on third base and clapped his hands like a maniac. "All right, all right, all right!" he yelled.

Robbie went out to have a chat with his pitcher. "You've thrown one tough ball game so far, Roger. Now ignore Jackson and concentrate on throwing strikes. All these guys standing behind you"—Robbie gestured toward his teammates in the field—"are all-stars. Whatever the West hits, they'll catch. Okay?"

Roger nodded, slapping the ball into the webbing of his glove. "Right," he said with new determination.

Bert Nagata had shaken the cobwebs out of his head and was now ready at third base. Robbie went back behind the plate. Roger Boyce looked in for the signal, saw it, and nodded. He unleashed a fast ball for a called strike.

The next two pitches, however, were just-missed strikes, bringing the count to 2–1. The West batter fouled off the fourth pitch for strike two. Then the fifth pitch dipped below the batter's knees for ball three. It was a full count now.

Roger Boyce peered in for the signal. Robbie called for a fast ball practically straight down the middle. Roger nodded and went into his wind-up. As he did, Jason Jackson stormed toward home from third base. All the runners were churning toward the next base now.

The fast ball came in high and tight, but the batter swung! Strike three! Robbie had to stand to catch the rising pitch.

161

Jason Jackson was now four feet from home plate. He was moving like a runaway train. Robbie braced himself. *Crunch!* The two catchers collided. Robbie was knocked backward five yards. Jackson was lying in a heap about a foot from home plate, out cold. Robbie's head slammed against the ground. He blacked out for two seconds. Roger Boyce had run in to cover home. When he saw Robbie might be dazed, he ran to grab the ball from him. The runner from second base was rounding third and heading for home!

Robbie came to, shaking his head, before Roger reached him. Robbie staggered up, then bolted toward the uncovered plate. The runner leapt headfirst over the motionless mountain of Jackson's body. Robbie jumped headfirst at the plate, stretching the ball in front of him for the tag. It caught the runner on his left hand as it reached toward the plate. Robbie's momentum carried him into the rest of the runner's body. They crashed in a heap on top of Jackson.

"Out!" yelled the umpire.

Jason Jackson suddenly groaned and sat up, tumbling the runner and Robbie off him. He looked around and blinked. "Am I in Oklahoma?" he asked.

The crowd went wild. First, the East fans were hollering and clapping for their team's spectacular victory. Then the whole stadium was applauding Robbie. He had just won the game for his team with an unassisted triple play!

The East players were cheering and congratu-

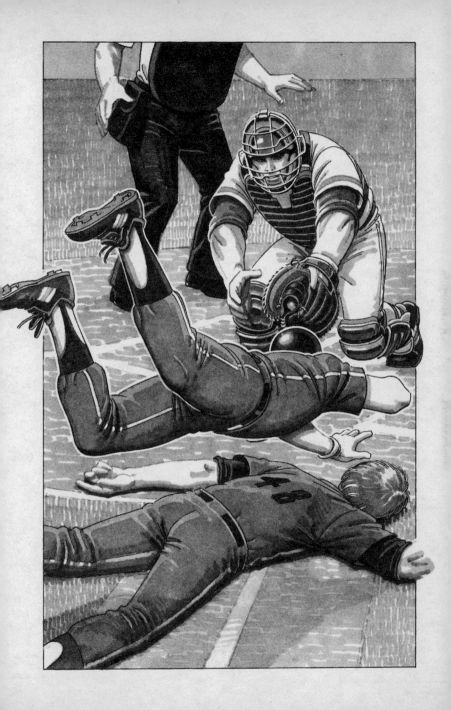

lating themselves. Once Robbie realized what had happened, he smiled. Then he walked straight over to the West team's dugout and shook Ace Mahoney's hand.

"Good game, Ace," he said.

"Thanks, Belmont. Looks like you had your own demolition derby at the plate. Are you okay?"

"Yeah, I guess."

"What're you doing next year?"

"College. Either Lansley or Redstone. Probably Lansley."

"Let me tell you, Belmont," said Ace, "Lansley's Harrington can be annoying, but he's one heck of a coach."

"I like Frank Preston better," said Anthony Sciannimanico, taking a seat next to Ace. "And Redstone University's terrific! You going there?"

"I don't know," said Robbie. "I don't think so."

"You'd better go join your team," said Ace. "But thanks for dropping by! You're a class act, Belmont."

"Thanks, Ace," said Robbie. "Good game again."

"Good? Yeah, I suppose. But yours was great."

Chapter Fifteen

There was renewed interest from the pro scouts in Robbie after his performance in the Johnston Senior All-American Game. He also received more than a few phone calls from assistant coaches on various college baseball teams around the country. Telegrams stacked on his bedroom desk practically shouted out for Robbie to accept a scholarship to this college or that.

Robbie knew that playing baseball at Lansley University would be closest to the life of a pro. The school calendar seemed to revolve around the extended Lansley baseball season. Head coach George Harrington always received plenty of press, and a good percentage of his players made the major leagues.

Robbie's friend, Ralph Butler, would be going to Lansley. Its track program was a close second to its baseball program. And Ralph had raved about the campus after visiting it. He said it was like paradise.

165

But that was before Riverton High School's principal had called Robbie into his office one afternoon. Also present were Coach Franklin and the school guidance counselor. The news was short and direct: Lansley University had no formal communications program at all! The new building Norman Taylor had mentioned a while ago was actually for the business school. The best Lansley could offer in communications were some speech and composition courses.

Redstone University, on the other hand, had a special, four-year program in communications. Included was a core of required writing, speech, and broadcasting courses, plus a host of elective courses. Redstone also had a brand-new television production studio now being used by its communications majors. And its small campus radio station provided hands-on training for those interested in a radio career.

All of this information made a strong impression on Robbie. He felt he had been misled by Lansley's Norman Taylor. But Robbie also knew he hadn't done his "homework" in checking out the school. The fault lay on both sides, he realized.

Now, sitting at his bedroom desk, Robbie was thinking of everything that was said in the principal's office that day. He shuffled the telegrams on his desk like a deck of cards. That's when he heard a light tapping on his bedroom door.

"Who is it?" he called softly.

Simon Belmont poked his head in. He was smiling as if he had a secret. "Something else for you in the mail today, son," he said. Simon handed Robbie a light green envelope. It smelled of perfume . . . a certain kind of perfume . . . the kind Cynthia Wu wore.

"Thanks, Dad," said Robbie, eagerly reaching for his letter opener.

"Don't mention it," said Simon, quietly leaving and closing the door.

Robbie read the handwritten letter slowly. He didn't want to miss a word, not even a comma.

Dear Robbie,

I've been meaning to write to you for weeks, but exams and term papers kept me pretty busy during April and May. Anyway, I read "Losing," the article you wrote for the high-school paper. Dennis sent it to me.

I really liked it. Without being preachy, it showed how to lose—and win—with a little dignity. I especially liked the way you described the Devon Wolverines' catcher coming over to shake your hand at the end of the state championship game. He could have kept celebrating on the field with his teammates, but instead he consoled you. It's a side of sports not often seen by people, and you wrote about it with a lot of feeling.

You have a real gift, Robbie. It's not just with a bat, ball, and glove, either. It's with words. You have to keep developing that. You have to!

Of course, who am I to be telling you

what to do? I know we haven't been getting along the last couple of times we've met. But I still think about you. And I miss you. One of the things I want more than anything right now is to get to know you better—*really* know you, what you think, how you feel.

How *do* you feel, Robbie? About me? Us? Is there an "us"?

Call. Soon.

Yours truly,
Cynthia

Yours truly, Robbie thought. *Cynthia. Don't I wish!*

He picked up his phone and tapped out Cynthia's number at Redstone University. He had it memorized. A strange woman's voice answered. She said she was a summer school student who had just moved into the dorm.

"Whoops! Sorry!" said Robbie. In his haste, he had forgotten that Redstone's spring semester was over. He hung up, then dialed Cynthia's home phone number.

"Hello?" It was Cynthia.

"Hi."

"Robbie! Ahhh—"

"I just got your letter. It was great. It made a whole lot of things click into place."

"Oh, uh, I'm glad," she said. "I didn't know how you'd react." She paused, then said, "Dennis told me about the all-star game. Way to go!"

"Thanks."

There was another pause. "Isn't there something you want to ask me, Robbie?"

"Uh, yeah, sure," he said. His mind deserted him. "Um, how did your final exams go?"

"That's not what I meant."

Finally, it occurred to Robbie. He smacked himself lightly on the forehead with his hand. "Say, I know it's kind of short notice. I mean, it's no notice, really. But would you like to go out tonight—with me?"

"What time?"

Robbie looked at the clock on his wall. "Oh, say, an hour from now?"

"Make it half an hour."

"Okay. Half an hour it is!"

"See you then."

"Right. Bye." Robbie was just about to hang up when he put the receiver to his mouth again. "Oh, Cynthia?"

"Yes?"

"I'm going to Redstone University." Robbie had decided the moment before he said it.

This time, there was a long silence on the other end of the phone. Robbie could only hear her breathing. That was all. Then, Cynthia spoke again. "I'm so glad, Robbie." The relief in her voice was unmistakable.

"You are? I mean, you are!" Robbie could barely contain his joy.

"Well, I have to go now," said Cynthia. "I'm

expecting a visit from a special guy soon." She gently hung up.

Robbie set his phone back in its cradle. *Redstone and Cynthia, here I come!* he thought to himself, slipping on his best shirt.

Behind the Iron Mask

Great baseball action and off-field drama
await you in all six of Gary Carter's Iron
Mask books. Future Hall of Famer Gary
Carter, a ten-time National League
selection as catcher for the annual All-
Star Game and the 1984 All-Star Game
MVP, has closely consulted on this
baseball series. And he has written a
personal introduction for each book.
Follow the exciting exploits of Iron Mask
series' hero Robbie Belmont as he rises
from high-school star...to college record
breaker...to promising pro!

Book #1: *Home Run!*
Book #2: *Grand Slam*
Book #3: *Triple Play*
Book #4: *MVP*
Book #5: *Hitting Streak*
Book #6: *The Show!*